STONE ARABIA

Also by Dana Spiotta

Lightning Field
Eat the Document

STONE ARABIA

DANA SPIOTTA

CANONGATE
Edinburgh · London

First published in Great Britain in 2012 by
Canongate Books Ltd, 14 High Street, Edinburgh EH1 1TE

1

First published in the Unites States of America in 2011 by
Scribner, a division of Simon & Schuster, Inc.,
1230 Avenue of the Americas, New York, NY 10020

British Library Cataloguing-in-Publication Data
A catalogue record for this book is available on
request from the British Library

ISBN 978 0 85786 373 7

Designed by Carla Jayne Jones

Printed and bound in Great Britain by
CPI Group (UK) Ltd, Croydon CR0 4YY

www.canongate.tv

This book is published on FSC certified paper

For Clem Coleman

The beauty for which I aim needs little to appear—unbelievably little. Anyplace—the most destitute—is good enough for it.

Jean Dubuffet, *Landscaped Tables,*
Landscapes of the Mind, Stones of Philosophy

I just wanna stay in the garage all night.

"Garageland," the Clash,
written by Mick Jones and Joe Strummer

STONE ARABIA

She always said it started, or became apparent to her, when their father brought him a guitar for his tenth birthday. At least that was the family legend, repeated and burnished into a shared over-memory. But she did really think it was true: he changed in one identifiable moment. Up until that point, Nik's main occupations had been reading *Mad* magazine and making elaborate ink drawings of dogs and cats behaving like far-out hipsters. He had characters—Mickey the shaggy mutt who smoked weed and rode motorcycles; Linda the sluttish afghan who wore her hair hanging over one eye; and Nik Kat, his little alter ego, a cool cat who played pranks and escaped many close calls. Nik Kat addressed the reader directly and gave little winky comments about not wanting you to turn the page. Denise appeared as Little Kit Kat, the wonder tot. She had a cape and followed all the orders Nik Kat gave her. Nik made a full book out of each episode. He would make three or four copies with carbon paper and then later make more at some expense at the print shop, but each of the covers was created by hand and unique: he drew the images in Magic Marker and then collaged in pieces of colored paper cut from magazines. Denise still had Nik's zines in a box somewhere. He gave one copy to her and Mom (they had to share), one to his girlfriend of the moment (Nik always had a girlfriend), one was put in a plastic sleeve and filed in his fledgling archives, and one went to their father, who lived in San Francisco.

Nik would take his father's issue, sign it, and write a limited-edition number on it before taping it into an elaborate package cut from brown paper grocery bags. He would address it to Mr. Richard Kranis. (Always with the word *Kronos* written next to it in microscopic letters. This alluded to an earlier time when each person in Nik's life was assigned the name and identity of a god. Naturally his dad was Kronos, and even though Nik had long ago moved on from his childish myths-and-gods phase, their father forever retained his Kronos moniker in subtle subscript.) Nik would draw all over the package, making the wrapping paper an extension of the story inside. After he mailed it off to his father, he recorded the edition numbers and who possessed them in his master book. Even then he seemed to be annotating his own life for future reference. "Self-curate or disappear," he would say when they were older and Denise began to mock him for his obsessive archiving.

Denise didn't think their father ever responded to these packages, but maybe he did. She never asked Nik about it. Her father would send a couple of toys in the mail for their birthdays, but not always, and not every birthday. She remembered him visiting a week after Christmas one year and bringing a carload of presents. He gave Denise a little bike with removable training wheels and sparkly purple handlebar tassels. But the most significant surprise was when he turned up for Nik's tenth birthday.

Nik and Denise lived on Vista Del Mar about two blocks from the Hollywood Freeway. Their mother rented a small white stucco bungalow. (In his comics Nik dubbed the house Casa El Camino Real, which later became Casa Real—pronounced "ray-al" or "reel," depending on how sarcastic you were feeling—and they found it forever amusing to always refer to it that way; eventually even their mother called it Casa Real. By the time Nik was in high school, he had become one of those people who gives names to everything: his car, his school, his bands, his friends. One who knew him well—say, Denise—could tell his mood by what nickname he used. The only things that didn't get nicknames were his guitars. They were referred to by brand names—the Gibson—or by categories—the bass—and never as, say, his *axe,* and he never gave them gender-specific pronouns, like "she's out of tune." Giving nicknames to his gear seemed unserious to him.)

When they first moved in to Casa Real, Nik had his own room while Denise shared a room with her mother. Later on Denise got Nik's room and Nik made the back dining room—with its own door leading outside—into his spacious master bedroom/smoking den/private enclave. Later still he would commandeer the entire garage. Nik stapled carpet remnants on the walls and made a soundproof recording and rehearsal studio.

For his tenth birthday, Nik wanted to go to the movies with a couple of friends and then have a cookout in the backyard with cake and presents. That was the plan. Nik wanted to see *Dr. Strangelove,* but Denise was too little, so they went to the Campus on Vermont Avenue to see the Beatles movie *A Hard*

Day's Night. Nik was a bit of a Beatle skeptic; he had the 45s, but he wasn't sure it wasn't too much of a girl thing. The movie erased all his doubt. Denise remembered how everything about it thrilled them—the music, of course, but also the fast cuts, the deadpan wit, the mod style, the amused asides right into the camera. The songs actually made them feel high, and in each instance felt permanently embedded in their brains by the second repetition of the chorus. They stayed in their seats right through the credits. If it wasn't for the party, there was no question they would have watched it again straight through.

When Denise reluctantly followed Nik out into the afternoon light, it shocked her to discover the world was just as they had left it. There it stood in hot, hazy, Beatle-free color. No speed motion and no guitar jangle. But it didn't matter, because they still had the songs in their heads, and they knew they would go to see the movie again as soon as they could. They took the bus to Hollywood Boulevard to look at records. Then they walked from Hollywood Boulevard up to Franklin, and Nik began to sing the songs from the film a cappella; he could perfectly mimic the phrasing of each Beatle vocal. Nik could also imitate the Liverpool accents, and he already knew some of the lines by heart (*We know how to behave! We've had lessons!*). They walked single file through the tunnel that went under the freeway (*He's very fussy about his drums, you know. They loom large in his legend*). Nik and Denise were still movie-drunk when they turned onto Vista Del Mar.

Their father's car sat in the driveway, a white Chrysler Imperial. Nik started to run down the block.

They found him in the backyard with their mother. He

hadn't brought his girlfriend, and he was wearing a sport coat even though it was very warm in the late-afternoon sun. Nik ran over to him and they hugged. Denise only stared at him. She was tiny for seven, with delicate features. She didn't look like a baby, but more like a perfect miniature girl. She hadn't seen her father in a long time, and she truthfully didn't feel very familiar around him. He got up and grabbed her around the waist with both hands. He was very tall. Denise would always have trouble remembering his face—she could see it in photographs, but she couldn't conjure it as it looked in real life. She could distinctly recall the feel of his hands gripping her. He lifted her up and squeezed her to his chest. Then he put her in the ledge of one bent arm and brushed her cheek with his hand. "Soft," he said, and grinned. In photos Denise's father looks like one of those character actors from the fifties: he is tall and broad and has exaggerated features. He is not unhandsome. He has clear olive skin and dense shiny black hair. But he also looks a little bloated around his eyes and nose, and he looks older than he should. Now when she studies photos of him, he appears to be a man well on his way to an early heart attack, a man who clearly ate and drank too much. But when he held her then, she noticed only how good he smelled, how big his body was. When he held you, he became your entire landscape. She felt shy, but she let him carry her, kiss her cheek, and gently tug her braids.

Nik and Denise would later agree that their father was awful. He randomly appeared and then one day he was just gone forever. "He would have been a great uncle," Nik said to her the last time they had discussed it. "The perfect present-carrying once-a-year uncle who can give you a report on how big you are and then wrestle with you for a minute before pouring himself a scotch and leaving the room." Their father left their mother when Nik was five, so he had some memories of living with him. Denise was two and had none. And before Nik turned eleven, their mother would wake them one Saturday morning and tell them their father had died. Nik would cry, sitting in his pajamas on the couch. Denise's mother also cried. Denise had to go to her room and stare at the picture she had of her father in her photo album. She really had to concentrate: He's dead, and I will never, ever see him again. And finally, staring at his photo, she, too, began to cry.

He couldn't stay for the birthday cookout. He was in town on business. "I wanted to surprise you," he said. "I'll just stay for a drink."

He sat in the sun and drank from a tumbler of ice and bourbon. He smoked a cigarette and sweated in the shadeless yard. He wore a big ring on his finger that caught the sun and sparkled. Nik and his friends drank Cokes and they spoke in embarrassed hushes, glancing at Nik's father. Their mother cooked the hamburgers on the grill. Denise urged Nik to open his presents.

"Not yet," her mother said, "after the cake."

"I have something you can open now," her father said. He got up with a smile and went through the gate to the front, where his car was parked. They all stared at the gate until he came back, lugging a large black leather guitar-shaped case. He carried it to where Nik stood and put the case on the grass in front of him. Nik stared down at it. Although he had given Nik nice gifts in the past, the size and weight of this gift indicated an extravagance beyond any they had previously experienced.

"Open it, son."

Nik unbuckled the case and hinged up the top. The lacquered rosewood gleamed in the sun. Their father reached down and pulled the guitar up with one hand on the neck and the other hand under the body. Mother-of-pearl was inlaid on the fingerboard between the frets, and there was matching inlay trim along the edge of the body and an inlay rosette around the sound hole. He handed it over to Nik, who pulled it to his chest. Nik stared down at it.

He finally spoke in a reverent whisper. "Thank you." And that was it.

THE CHRONICLES

July 1, 2004

Dear Ada,

It is nearing midnight, and I can't wait to leave this travesty of a day behind. It was not good or happy or kind. It took a long time to get here, and it will take a long time to leave. Be warned, I feel disoriented. But I will proceed in the finest faith I can muster. I must take care. Because, as we know, memory all too easily accommodates the corruption of regret.

You may surmise that I have had something to drink. This might make you think I am being hyperbolic or histrionic or that word that makes all women of my age cringe, hysterical. As if my hormones or my uterus (the Greek word for womb is hustera, etc.) were the engine of my writerly ablutions. That's not it. Mostly I am writing because I know and see things no one else does. Because I have to. It is my job, my assignment. I am on the verge of elation. Liberated. Part of me feels relief, I cannot deny it.

I will elaborate, I promise.

"Oh, for God's sake," Denise said, barely audible in the empty room. Is this really what she was left with? Another overly elaborated joke?

How peculiar this feels: before tonight I never imagined I would try to write about anything, much less this. I don't mean I don't understand why people write. Written words demand the deep attention that spoken words just aren't entitled to. Writers get to pull something solid out of our relentless, everyday production of verbal mucilage. A writer is a word salvager and scavenger and distiller.

As you know, I have occasionally fixated on words—I love to talk and sometimes words come out with embarrassing urgency. I can feel them as almost physical things as I push breath into them. This, I am afraid, is a consequence of solitude. Spoken words become extravagant and magical, and I admit that I have, on more than one occasion, caught myself speaking my thoughts aloud, as though vocalizing them gave them an extra reality, but I don't think I ever felt any urgent expressive needs about actually writing words down. No desire to extrude something that would endure beyond my mere mortal squeak. Except now, when writing them down seems not to be about cheating the given human terms but instead simply a way to relieve my isolation. "The artistic impulse," wrote Colette, "even more than the sexual impulse, breaches the barriers." So be it—smash these walls down. Raze them to the cellar.

Denise stopped reading and took a long breath. And then another. She swayed and steadied herself against her brother's desk. She realized she had been holding her breath as she read. And standing. She pulled out his desk chair with her elbow. She did not put the letter down. She held it in her hand, her index finger and middle finger keeping the last page distinct from the first. She sat on his chair and leaned toward his desk.

Her damp hair stuck to the back of her neck. She should take a sip of water, something. Denise read on to see what Nik had "Denise" say next.

The simplest answer and probably the most accurate answer is that Nik's art was his life. And I don't know what that means about a life. I have always resisted artistic impulses of any kind. I always believed that if you weren't good, what right did you have to do it? This question dates back to when I did try, for a time, to be an actress. A deliverer and even exalter, I imagined, of all those delightfully rescued and worked words, phrases, and sentences. At seventeen I even enrolled in a very exclusive acting workshop. You didn't know this, did you? But I must confess my initial appearance there, like many things in my life, was accidental. The class met at an equity-waiver theater on Melrose Avenue every Wednesday night. He was a famous teacher; he coached serious movie actors. He would be hired to be on set during important scenes. He held secrets, we were led to believe. And despite how cliché this may sound, I was not even intending to audition for his class. I was there with a friend who wanted to audition. My friend Avril (who burned to be an actor from the moment she saw Judith Anderson's repulsive-yet-compelling performance in Hitchcock's brilliant domestic torture film Rebecca*), wanted to go and I came along to help her. We did a scene from* Done by Hand. *I played Janice. I knew nothing about acting. I had no desire to act. But, in the same way a broken clock is right twice a day (I apologize for another cliché), anyone can act for one scene if the one scene happens to require the exact comportment with which you are naturally inclined to when on stage. So in this specific role, in this specific scene, my fontal rush of propulsive fear,* *my prickly self-strickenness, and my strangled underlaugh that was (and still is) a result of what Sigmund Freud identified as the "liminal dilemma between the intense desire for supplication and the concurrent need for masochistic provocation" all combined to create an illusion of a brilliant stage presence, bursting with potential and future possibility. All of which I didn't have—not as an actor, certainly.*

So I was astonishing, a dazzling creature of tangled, alluring complexity. For five minutes, at seventeen, in the Barbara Stanwyck Theater on a Wednesday.

I said my last line, blurted it in a manic breath. I heard the famous teacher say, "Stop there." I felt dampness leaking under my arms; I was glistening with what I would have guessed is called "flop sweat"; I could even feel a trickle down the side of my neck. I opened my eyes (they must have been closed for the entire last line). Avril stared at me, her lips quivering. Her face was red and she was clearly on the verge of tears. Was I that bad? I could feel the whole room on the edge of a deep intake of breath, and then into the breach came an avalanche of intense applause. What a thing, Ada. The rough din of all that sudden hand-smacking: you actually can feel it as well as hear it. It is an assault; it is as if they are trying to break in to you somehow. They are laying a claim to whatever it is you just created. I nearly fainted.

The teacher appeared out of the dark and mounted the stage. He waved his hand at the audience and the applause abruptly stopped. His face betrayed no apparent pleasure or displeasure: it was a studious, controlled expression. (One should expect nothing less from an acting teacher than control of the face.) Then I realized his intent, his concentration, was fixed. And it was not fixed on

Avril; it was fixed on me. I was along to merely assist, but I was asked to join the workshop on the spot and Avril was not.

Looking back, I must concede there was a little more to it than my coincidental impersonation of a gifted actor. The more to it that I am alluding to is the way I looked. This is a sketchy thing to discuss, but I was frankly pretty in a very actressy way. I had that extra-pretty shine that seems to fix to actors, a shimmery charisma that you can't miss even if the actor has unwashed hair and no makeup on. I saw Cary Grant, once, at the Beverly Center on a Saturday afternoon. He was silver-haired, way past his heyday. Yet he was that extra-shiny thing, a gorgeous old man, not at all like anyone else there. What is more, he seemed to suck up all the attention in the place, he was like a black hole, drawing curiosity and desire like matter toward infinity. And it had nothing to do with fame, at least not for me, because I didn't even recognize him. I noticed him before I saw everyone whispering and I discovered who he was. A young woman pushed the shopping cart as he strolled alongside; he appeared conspicuously unaware of the gaze of others as he attended a cantaloupe with an outstretch of his cashmere-covered arm. His power came from his electric prettiness, his extra glow. If we were all in a painting, he would have one of those intricate halos around him, gilt-traced, radiant. That's exactly what it was, a radiance that felt holy. At least as holy as one could feel shopping at the Beverly Center on a Saturday afternoon. I nearly stopped and applauded as he walked by. We all nearly did.

My extra-prettiness was a minor version of that. I had the regular, symmetrical features of a pretty girl. I had the slim yet plush figure of the standard object of desire. And on top of that I had this little sparkly extra thing, the thing that makes people think you ought to be an actor, the thing that makes everyone sneak disbelieving glances at every detail of you. (Does the exquisite hollow of her philtrum meet her lip at exactly the most alluring depth? Yes, it does. Do her tiny pale earlobes hang only halfway before attaching in the most elegant and demure way? Oh yes. And so on.) I still have some remnant of that kind of beauty, but even I know that it really peaked for me at around seventeen. Some women grow into their peak beauty: they are deep, powerful creatures. Some women seem to miss it entirely, the sum of their pieces becoming somehow less than is really fair. My mother was in the latter category. Her attractiveness had always felt unrealized. She was fifteen pounds away, or she needed a new haircut, or clothes that fit her better. But that was an illusion. She just didn't add up in quite the right way, and no matter what she did, there would always be something just out of reach for her. She was a woman who always appeared past her peak but who actually never had a peak. And then other women, like me, peak very early. It is a subtle distinction. I mean, I was still quite pretty at twenty-five. I am still reasonably, wearily pretty at forty-seven. (Way prettier than I need to be, especially now that I am a writer.) But when I was on stage at the Barbara Stanwyck Theater, in that audition for that very exclusive acting workshop, it was natural for people to mistake me for a born-to-be-a-star type. I looked like someone whose fabulous peak was yet to come. (Because what peak beauty ever reads like a peak? It must all be becoming, it must all be a leap into the future for a woman.)

He, the famous teacher Herbert Mintov, stopped the applause and we all stood there. He ignored Avril and looked into my face. I remember he cupped my face with his hands, but I am sure that can't be right. That would be creepy. Herbert was full of all sorts of character flaws, but he would never have made the mistake of appearing creepy. So he didn't actually touch me, but he did something that was an appropriate teacherly version of that, something along the lines of opening a hand toward me, nodding sagely at me, and saying I was invited to join the class. As I recall, nothing was said to Avril, and so it was with the brutal terms of the acting world. How could I refuse? I had no idea what I was going to do in this life. When you grow up in Los Angeles, sooner or later it occurs to you that acting could be your calling. Especially if you were more or less recruited, Schwab's-style, into the thing.

As you might have guessed, my acting career went steeply, vertiginously downhill from that first brilliant peak. Herbert's mistake soon became clear to me, Herbert, and the other students. (But not Avril, of course, because we were no longer friends. She was convinced, and she could have been right, that I upstaged and displaced her. That she never had a shot. Which might have been true, but it certainly wasn't on purpose. And my refusing Herbert's invitation would not have furthered her cause in any way, that was clear. I do think it gives the lie to one acting cliché: it isn't true that if you surround yourself with brilliant actors you will only look better. What is true is you will look weaker. All other actors are your enemy, tarnishing and interrogating your aura of holy radiance. What you need is to be surrounded by serviceable, competent journeymen. Avril learned that and so did I.)

I hate, so deep in this little digression, to insert yet another actor cliché, but if I'm here for anything, it is for truth, for disclosure, for the full story, no matter how tacky that full story might make me seem. It will all, in the end, figure in to the decisions I have made recently. All mistakes lead to further mistakes: all we can do is make a plausible, causal accounting. And maybe I can be excused for the predictable trajectory of my actor's journey. Here it is: I did have an affair with Herbert. Of course I did.

But I really should get back to the story of Nik, I should have said how all of this pertained to Nik. Nik, unlike me, never had a doubt about who he was or what he wanted to do. He didn't wait for people to tell him what he was good at. He didn't just go along with some authority figure the way I just joined Herbert's acting class because I was invited. I don't think you could flatter Nik into doing something he didn't feel all the way through him. But me, I had to say yes to Herbert's offer, and then I had to sleep with Herbert, too. I don't need to invite your disgust by going into the details of our lurid assignations. I did start it, I think it is important to be truthful about who initiated things. I knew Herbert wanted me, that was obvious. So I started an affair with him because I felt sorry for him. I was such a terrible actress, he was so completely wrong about my potential, and there he was, stuck with me in class. I brought the whole place down. I was so stiff and self-conscious on stage that I made everyone—all these talented, ambitious actors—hate acting. They would watch me do a scene, and they would think: I hate acting, I hate actors. I quit. I know this was how they felt when they watched me. When you aren't good at something, you just make everyone despair about anything ever being good again. That is why Gertrude Stein said "Bad art smells human in all the wrong ways." And bad stage acting is the worst of all—you are stuck right in the room with the embarrassment of the actor's failure. You become a party to the failure. And there I was, in this room full of very talented actors, actors who could take you to the depths of anyone's soul. Actors willing to enliven the most hated skins, actors capable of impersonating—of infusing personhood into—whatever words some dark little writer piled up on a page. And they did it with flesh and spirit, they did it with breathing, they did it with finely elucidated human detail. These actors were Zen geniuses, selfless beings capable of both extreme control and fearless spontaneity. They could listen and react to each other, and yet they were disciplined in their devotion to text and coherence. They observed every little self-revealing tic and gesture. They had such endless insight into the compelling whys and ways of human behavior. They prized the integrity of the souls they created; they were fearless.

Except, of course, when they watched me.

Or even worse, when they had to perform with me. I embodied their rediscovered fear. As the class continued, my bad acting became more and more elaborated and intricate. I have to be exact about this—if there is any possible accomplishment in these sentences, it dwells in exactitude. So here is not just how bad I was but how I was bad: I wasn't lazy. I memorized my lines (by rote and repetition, by groping, by blind will). I wrote notes in the margins. I thought of Motivations. Objectives. Actions. As-ifs. I dutifully penciled them in. I had, I believe, deep insight into the characters I was assigned. I would go to the library and do research. When I was supposed to have pleurisy, I read every detail of what pleurisy does to you (it creates a heaviness in your lungs, labored breathing, and knifelike cutting pain in your chest). I read about the Depression. I read about St. Louis. I worked hard at my acting. I am, if nothing else, an extremely hard worker. I have always worked hard because I have always had to.

You must understand something: Nik and I went to crowded urban public schools. We lacked supervision, parental or any other kind. Necessarily, our education was an act of autocarpy. We didn't know a thing we didn't teach ourselves. Nik found a way to revel in his self-conjured education and even saw it as his strength. As the twelfth-century literary genius Abu Jaafar Ebn Tophail wrote in his primordial epic novel, Philosophus Autodidactus: *"The feral child will develop the purest form of creativity." But for me it was different: my feral childhood left me hounded by doubt. When you are self-taught, you get a lot of things wrong. You mispronounce words because you never actually heard anyone speak those words aloud. You use what linguists call hypercorrect language that is in fact not correct, like sticking* whom *all over the place. Or you use the first-person subjective pronoun* I *even when you should use the first-person objective pronoun* me *because you think the word* me *is only for selfish children. You try to never say the word* like, *because you can't be sure how to do it without thinking about it. You learn to second- and triple-guess your instincts, which can really change how you make your way through the world. You are slow because you have to take the long way around to everything. No utterance comes without labored preparations. None of this weighed on Nik, but I always found it humiliating that I didn't even know what I didn't know. So my hard work, unlike Nik's, was underwritten by a kind of despair. I worked desperately hard, you see? I couldn't give up. I was determined to at least be a rigorous failure.*

Herbert did try his best with me. He patiently and clearly expounded the techniques of controlling your body as an actor. I did his Movement exercises. I did his Breathing exercises. I did Sense-Memory exercises. I hummed, I shook out my limbs, I pliéd.

But.

Nothing could override my continuing and enduring awfulness. For all of my efforts and Herbert's efforts, I actually started to get worse. But that isn't exactly true. I couldn't have gotten worse, that wasn't possible; it was just the longer my attempts at acting went on, the more hopeless it felt to do it. My actual performances were strikingly consistent and uniform: I would get on stage with all of my hard work behind me. I would carry it all out there. I didn't go blank or anything like that. Here is precisely what happened every time: nothing. I couldn't take all that underlife, all that between-the-lines annotation, all that hard-willed work and alchemize it into any felt thing. I couldn't feel. I couldn't make anyone else feel. As Herbert said once, in exasperation (in bed, actually, after we had had perfectly fine sex), "It is make-believe, don't you get it? You just have to make me believe. You can get away with whatever you want if you can make me believe it." Which I couldn't do, and Herbert could not teach me. I thought of it all, I even thought of not thinking, but I felt nothing, convinced no one. At last I quit. When I finally told him I was done with it, I didn't just feel relief, I felt a deep release, a reprieve from being so horribly bad.

But now I understand that I had it all wrong. The issue isn't, Am I good enough? No. The issue is, Do I not have any other choice? Will and desire don't matter. Ability doesn't matter. Need is the only thing that matters. I need to do this.

Enough, Ada darling. I'm way off subject and I don't seem to have managed my task very well. You will say, You haven't explained, why didn't you do something if you knew? And you are right, I did know. And you are wrong, I shouldn't and couldn't have stopped anything. I will try to make you see that. I will try again after I sort things out. And Ada, despite my rambling and middling self-recriminations, don't—please don't—pity me. Or Nik. As Gloria Steinem once said, "Pity is simply hate without the respect."

Yours always,
Ma

Denise stuck the letter back in the envelope glued to the page under the taped-in, cut-out typed heading *July 1, 2004.* This was not a letter from Denise to her daughter, Ada. It was a sham, a hoax, a put-on. This document was from Nik's Chronicles. Denise found it there, as she was meant to. This was a letter, written by her brother, in her style—or his conjured style of her—for his Chronicles. He did a rather fascinating and painful facsimile of Denise, a witty, brutal parody of her. For her, actually, because Denise was pretty much the main audience for the Chronicles (besides Nik himself, of course). He exaggerated her pretensions, her diction, her grating trebly qualities. He made fun of her memory skills. (Denise took supplements to aid memory. She did brain exercises. She convinced herself that her ability to remember was speedily evaporating.) She pressed her hand against the open binder. She smoothed the page and could feel the weight and chunked thickness of all the pasted-in entries. The sun had come up, she could see a faint glow at the seams of the garage door and in the small row of windowpanes. She should call someone. What would she say? She tucked the open binder under her arm and climbed up the ladder through the trapdoor to Nik's apartment. She made a cup of coffee with Nik's plug-in percolator. She pulled back the black curtain on one of the east-facing windows. The pink edges of the dawn made the scrubby desert oaks look carved in light. It was very quiet. No coyotes or cars. She sat down at his desk with her cup of coffee and pulled the volume of the Chronicles toward her. She took the faux letter out and read it again.

He didn't really exaggerate her digressive tendencies, she couldn't argue with that. All that ridiculous acting stuff. She had taken one acting class and she wasn't that bad. She was commonplace bad. She was much more commonplace in all respects than this Denise-on-steroids that Nik created for the Chronicles, which she knew was never meant to be about the facts or actual life out in the world.

As for the fake quotes, she got a kick out of those. That was Nik's signature affectation for her, his marker of anything rendered in her voice. The made-up quotes were her attributes, like Saint Lucy always appearing with her eyes on a plate, but the reference was only understood by Denise, only really understood in the context of the entire Chronicles, and so, finally, a profoundly elaborated private joke between them.

What was he getting at with some of this? Nik threw little pebbles and they pinged against the glass; his versions of the two of them kept very close in their own weird-logic way. There was no question that she would have to call Ada next. She would have to account for her actions—or lack thereof—to Ada. She must delineate, with some exactitude—as he ironically put it in his fake letter—the truth of their sadness and troubles.

It was also accurate to say that Nik reveled in his solitude and Denise did not. She figured that was the first thing that separated them—that and when she began to become his audience. It wasn't just that Nik got a guitar from their father. Nik took it, grabbed hard at it, and never let it go. They diverged early, and after that there was no changing or stopping him.

From where she sat at his worktable, Denise could see his original guitar perched on a stand in the corner. An Orlando with a rosewood body "just like a Martin." Nik had taken good care of it. She knew he felt there was some destiny to the day he received it: the Beatles, the guitar, the last time they would see their father. She knew because Nik felt there was destiny in everything. The story was part of his legend: he hadn't even wanted a guitar—it never occurred to him, he would claim with a laugh. And yet it changed his life. Which was true, it did change him. It took him over like a disease. From that very evening he would not quit with that Orlando.

He used to sit by his record player and listen over and over to the same song until he figured out how to play a particular lead. He didn't read music or learn music theory. But Nik had a capacity for dogged devotion. He was doglike, really, the way a dog will chase a car it can never catch or will never tire of retrieving a ball you throw. He would come home from school or a party or a date, and he would automatically pick up his guitar, in just the same kind of habitual and nearly compulsive way Ada would run to her computer. Many times Denise remembered trying to tell Nik something and he would still be playing his guitar, working something out with fingers and string. It irritated her, the way he would sit there, then say, *Yeah*? And nod as she spoke, but still stealing glances downward, his left hand depressing strings, his right hand clutching a pick, just touching the pick to strings without strumming. He was showing Denise this great amount of attention and respect by not actually strumming. She said, one time when she really wanted him to listen, "Could you just put your guitar down?" and he looked at her as if she'd asked him to put his arm down.

As it turned out, he was not the world's most brilliant guitar player. He was good, good enough for songwriting and singing, which were the things he really cared for. He worked at learning the guitar and achieved a high level of competence. Nik taught himself everything about playing, even taught himself the fact that he was not ever going to be a virtuoso.

The actual demise of Nik as possible guitar hero came in 1973. Nik had just begun to play out with his new band, the Demonics. Previously there had been some jam sessions with school friends, but the Demonics were his first band to venture past the garage. He had a bass player, Sam Stone, and a drummer, Mike Summer. (Or maybe it was Dave Winton first and Mike later?) They had scored a regular gig opening for bands at this shitty club called the Well. They played early in the evening when no one was really there, kind of a fill-in thing. But it was a great opportunity—they were just beginners. They still had these long shags and they were a little pimply and peeled. Nik was always pretty good-looking, but he hadn't found his look quite yet—he was still in the developmental stages. He was on the verge of good-looking. Denise went to all of the gigs even though she was sixteen and well under the legal age. She just slipped in as part of the group. She found a perch near the stage and folded her legs and arms until she felt nearly invisible. The Demonics played the same ten songs over and over. Although Nik had already written hundreds of songs by this point, the only ones they had rehearsed and could even play at all were these ten fairly simple songs. After a few weeks of their boring set, Nik tried to introduce new songs. But something wasn't working. They would just fade on the stage, already sick of themselves. Then they would get some minuscule amount of money and mope around the edge of the performance area. They'd stay for the next band if they could, but the club knew the Demonics were all underage and they weren't supposed to hang out after the gig. One night, though, they did manage to stay for the next band, the Cherries. There were four of them—drums, bass, and two guitars. They all had short hair (for that time) and wore collared, short-sleeved tennis shirts buttoned all the way up and tucked in to their beltless, tight, flat-front khaki pants. Nobody looked like that yet.

"Speed preps," Nik whispered, staring at them. The singer hardly touched his guitar and spent most of his time closed-eyed at the mic, hurling words into the dark. He would hold a chord and then wave his right hand at the strings at crucial moments, giving an underfill to their sound. The other guitar player, the taller, sweatier one, played the leads and sometimes sang harmony—his singing kicked in about as often as the lead singer swiped at his guitar. They played seven hard, fast, close rockers. They wiped the Demonics off the stage. Nik knew it, Denise could tell by how he studied them.

From that moment on, he focused on his songwriting. He recruited Tommy Skate to play lead guitar for his shows. *And the rest was history.* He understood he wasn't ever going to be one of those great live guitar players, no matter how hard he worked on it. He didn't spend forever flogging his failures. He moved things along. Denise slowly began to realize how deeply serious he was.

The Demonics grew to be a pretty decent live band. But Nik preferred composing to performing. He never stopped writing new songs. As devoted as he had been to learning the guitar, his obsession with songwriting trumped everything. He wrote in notebooks, he wrote while he watched TV, and yes, he wrote even while someone was trying to talk to him.

"Yeah," he said, nodding, but with that dazed noncommittal style the true nonlistener adopts. *I'm agreeing with you—just a crapshoot, but why not?* But Denise knew the songs were really good, so she couldn't mind all that much. She figured that's just how artists were.

The amazing thing was Nik didn't seem to pay attention to anyone or anything around him and yet then he would write something that seemed entirely to depend on the closest attention. Like "Versions of Me," his great early song about playing poseur and then wondering why no one knew the real you. He already let the ironic twist come in, the self-admonishment that made him such an appealing songwriter. When he first played this song for Denise, they were sitting in the kitchen of Casa Real. It was late, they had been out at a party. Denise followed Nik in, drunkenly shushing each other even though their mother was still out on a late shift and they were the only ones home. Denise walked straight to the pantry and took out a box of Wheat Thins. She stood with the pantry door open and gnashed a steady stream of salty squares between her teeth. This was her strategy to avoid room spins and subsequent hangovers. She always crammed as many starches in her stomach as she could before she made any attempts to go horizontal. And she always woke up sixteen and fresh-faced.

Nik held his guitar by the neck as he hoisted himself up on the old aquamarine tiled counter. He rested the guitar against his lap and attempted to reach in his jacket pocket for his cigarettes—he shifted his pick to teeth and tried again. He then replaced the pick with a cigarette and started to play. Denise didn't stop eating her crackers as she walked over to the narrow transom window above the sink and pushed it open.

"I'm not gonna smoke it," he said without looking up. She put her hand in the Wheat Thins box again and watched him strum. "You want to hear a new song?" he said, looking up. She nodded, leaning against the sink. He began to play "Versions of Me," and all at once Denise's very familiar but distant brother became someone else. This was truly the moment when she saw how different he was from everyone else she knew, including herself. He, just by singing his song, could change how she saw the world. He became a vivid human to her, someone who understood her as yet unnamed alienation. She had, all at once, a deep faith in his perception, as he pinpointed the way she often felt, angry at the world for misunderstanding her while playing at deliberately misrepresenting herself. He stopped and shrugged. He lit his cigarette and took a long, proud drag.

Brother is a rock star.

"I love it. It's great!" she said, still chewing.

He smiled.

"Your first hit!"

"A chart-topper," Nik said, with a sarcasm about his chances at success that would soon be replaced with something more, well, unusual.

The moment stood out to Denise for other reasons as well. She realized then that he was good at this, songwriting, in a way he never was at guitar playing. He had figured this out, while she was still nowhere.

Denise really should call someone.

She sat down at Nik's worktable, a huge unfinished piece of wood set on two sawhorses and pushed against the wall. His razor-point black pens of various widths and sharpened General's Cedar Pointe pencils were neatly lined up. Scissors, X-Acto blades, erasers, homemade wheat paste, double-sided photo tape, rubber cement, and Tombow Mono Adhesive were all within reach. A ream of acid-free pure white paper, and off to the side the white Royal manual typewriter with the lazy *a* that he used to type his formal entries in the Chronicles. Evidence of the Chronicles was everywhere around her. The earlier volumes were shelved in chronological order starting in the garage downstairs (1970s–2003). But he kept the volumes of the current year in a neat row on a shelf above his desk. On the walls near the desk she could see the framed album covers, posters, master images for label art, photos, and pasted-up fake news clippings. And under her hands and all in front of her was Nik's clear, inviting wood desk. All set up for work.

His archive oppressed her. She needed a chronicle of her own, with her own opposite silly penchant for reality and memory and ordinary facts. Because that was all she could think to do with what had transpired. She must conclude it liberated her in some deep way, and maybe it even did.

THE COUNTERCHRONICLES

My disclaimer:

You can go back forever to grab a context for a brother and sister. And even then the backward glance is distorted by the lens of the present. The further back, the greater the distortion. It is not just that emotions distort memory. It is that memory distorts memory, if that makes any kind of sense. I must simply try to recall the events that led to our crisis (let's call it that for now). Because there were contributing factors, things that speak to states of mind. There were signs and indications and decisions with consequences well before the events of the last few days. Can one make causal connections without manufacturing narratives? Or is all memory simply the application of narrative to past events, and is it only human and coherent to do that work? To begin, I must be quite clear with myself. I must do my best to stick to the fairly recent past, without the nostalgic digressions, to stick to exactly what happened this year, 2004, what actually happened to us, and, well, to me.

DECEMBER 31, 2003–JANUARY 1, 2004

I arrived at Nik's bar shortly before midnight. I call it Nik's bar, but it isn't. It is Dave's Bar. This marginal establishment—broken stools, gum-stuck linoleum floor tiles, dirty bathrooms, expensive speaker system, heavy pours—has been a functioning bar for three decades, with Nik working there, on and off, for most of those years. While the New Year announced itself in beer and blurry kisses, I sat, on my own, on the other side of the bar from Nik. (It is easy to recall the start of the year because of the holiday. A holiday helps to place you. Memory technique #1, use Dates as Placeholders in your brain. All calendars are simply ancient arbitrary mnemonic tools for the culture. We will take Pope Gregory's version and move on.) Naturally 2004 was a leap year—already a bad sign, as far as I was concerned, and I was deeply concerned. New Year's Eve is a rough holiday even in the best of years. 2004 whiffed bad from the get-go.

At midnight Nik would put on the Rolling Stones' "Dead Flowers." The song is easy to recall because he played it every year at midnight. Which also makes the actual night difficult to recall, as all the moments hearing that song run into one another, indistinct, uniformly soundtracked. He poured some drinks.

He keyed up the song. He poured himself a drink. He let the bar crowd start counting down the seconds until midnight. He poured more drinks. It is just a sloggy old bar, so mostly it was beer and shots and not a lot of complicated cocktails, but this year I saw he struggled to get all the rounds done in time so he could attend to the music and the countdown. He did this and I watched him, sort of hoping to talk for a moment. Although I hadn't had much to drink, I was feeling a little sentimental about my big brother. I had listened to his latest CD, a seasonal release called *Caroles and Candles* by his band the Pearl Poets. The Pearl Poets were a side project of Nik's in which he used the one-name pseudonym Mason. They were a moody folk trio—Mason, Mark, and Chris—but actually all of the parts were voiced by Nik. They all lived together at Tottenham Cottage in North London. They sang pristine Celtic-style layered harmonies, Nik managing all of this with his old Tascam four-track. The first Pearl Poets album, *Sylvan Shine,* was released in 1980. It was a concept electric folk record. All the songs on that album had sky-related titles: "Aurora Borealis," "Corona," "Fata Morgana," "Airglow," "Brocken Bow," etc. The second album, *Suites for the Sweet,* took ten years to produce. It featured original and traditional folk songs with electric arrangements. As I recall from the liner notes, Nik used lots of fiddle and unusual time signatures. I didn't think it was nearly as good as the first one. This current seasonal release of obscure traditional carols and a few original ballads was the third Pearl Poets album, and although the concept was a bit stretched at this point, it had been so many years since the last one it seemed fresh. A reunion Christmas album to cash in, I guess, was how he would describe it in the Chronicles. I loved it, and I was eager to report the details of my admiration. At least a superficial report, a first pass at it. But he was busy, and then we were right up against midnight. He drank his shot, "Dead Flowers" came on, the whole bar started singing along. He gave me a sloppy kiss on the cheek, his lips wet with bourbon, and I waited until he turned back to the bar before I wiped the wetness off my cheek with a bar napkin, quickly, and then returned the napkin to the bartop, where it found a wet spot and began to darken.

I suppose as I sat there in the early-morning hours of 2004 I might have been contemplating the previous year. I probably couldn't recall much—now I can't even recall if I recalled much. But my memory concerns hadn't reached their peak yet. My semi-obsessive interest in how my own memory functions would top out about a month later. All of that had begun with my mother's memory issues, which had really kicked in in the last few months of 2003.

Maybe, though, as I sat at the bar, I thought of Ada, and maybe I tried to picture her in New York, at a party. Which would have been nice. But sooner or later I have little doubt that my thoughts turned to my mother's mind. It is the kind of thing that occurs to you in the marginal moments of your life: during a commercial, a shower, in the fraught minutes before you fall asleep. Or when you sit at a bar, waiting for an arbitrary holiday marker to pass. You suddenly remember how badly she was failing and it deflates you, just takes the air right out of you. So I was probably thinking of her mind and memory, but I can't be sure, because I cannot recall anything except the song and the kiss and the cocktail napkin on the bar.

This is one of the reasons I am so squeamish about looking back. Can I even do it? Can I be accurate at all? I have discovered how much memory can dissolve under pressure. The more I try to hold on to my ability to remember, the more it seems to escape my grasp. I find this terrifying. I have become alarmed at my inability to recall basic facts of the past, and I have worked to improve things. I have been studying various techniques and even tricks, and I should employ them. Memory, it seems, clings to things. Named things. Spaces. Senses. I even tried the old trick (memory technique #2, use Rhyme and Stories) where you apply a little poem to things you want to remember. A little nonsense thing, like *His name is Ed and his nose is red.* Or Bob's birthday is 11-9-63, '63 is when Kennedy died, 119 is 911 backward. So *Kennedy's assassination was an emergency* is what you have to remember. And truly this stuff works, somehow giving your brain little games of association to help it organize its input. But there are two problems with this: I don't want to fill my head with stupid games. In the time it takes to think up this stuff, I mean, your life is going by. I just hate it too much, I'll just write down Bob's birthday, seriously. And that is the other problem. I don't want to remember someone's name or some date. That is the kind of skill a politician needs so he can be fast with hundreds of names. That is an imprinting technique for the future. I'm not interested in that (there are only a handful of names in my life). I'm thinking about past events. I'm interested in recall, exact recall, of what was said, who said it and to whom. I want to know the truth, undistorted by time and revision and wishes and regrets.

Shortly after midnight, Nik did not notice the now smushy

bar napkin or the wet spot it indicated. He lit a cigarette and leaned on the ledge of the back bar. He still had all his hair and he could shake it from his eyes, and I guess that made him seem youthful at first. But a closer look revealed how not-young he had become. As he inhaled, he squinted and his face revealed every frown and grimace he had ever made, every cigarette he had ever smoked. He hunched in his black T-shirt and his thin body humped at his belly. It looked as though a tight wedge of flesh had been appended to his middle. He still had muscle tone in his skinny-guy arms, but his sloped posture, which in the past gave him a blasé and phlegmatic glamour, now simply accentuated his paunch. He did not care, or seemed not to care, about his drinking belly or his general, considerable decay. He did not care that his hands shook when he lit his cigarette. He did not care when his conversation was brought to a halt by a coughing fit. He pursued a lifetime of abuse that could only come from a warped relationship with the future. Although I can't say my brother didn't believe in the future, I know he was never concerned with it. But for me sitting there, watching and thinking—now I remember—of my earlier visit to our mother, I didn't like it one bit. It was not pleasant New Year's contemplation for me. I was irritated by it, by him, and by the fact that the bar was wet and messy. I took the remnant of the napkin and sopped it around. He picked up a bar towel and wiped in front of me, an automatic and long-engrained bartender gesture. The bar towel smelled strongly of bleach and beer.

"I have to call Ada," I said, and got up from the bar.

"Tell her—"

"Yeah, I will."

I went to the side door of the bar and stepped into the sudden quiet—the almost ringing quiet—of the alley.

I'd missed a call from Jay. It was eight a.m. in England. Very, very sweet. I didn't listen to his message. I called Ada instead.

"Hey, Ma."

"It's Mom." I couldn't get used to people knowing who I am when I call.

"Yes—"

"Happy New Year, angel."

January first continued after I slept for a while; I got up by six-thirty, as it seemed indecent to sleep late on the very first day of a new year. I drank a full deep cup of coffee and then cleaned the house, easy enough to remember because I always spend New Year's Day cleaning the house. But again, habits and patterns also make this New Year's Day hard to distinguish from other New Year's Days, which were also spent cleaning, at least going back as far as when Will left. And even then it was the same, a deep day of cleaning, except Will would be there, so it would be a very different memory and not easily confused with these later, solitary New Year's Days.

The cleaning was pleasant and ruthless: I emptied the refrigerator of every object, the jar of butter-flecked jelly, the container of capers floating in leaky brine, the optimistic bottle of multivitamins now in a moist, smelly clump, even a not very old bottle of expensive flaxseed oil. All must go, and so it was easy, just dumping without having to smell or decide anything. I did the same thing in the bathroom, though not quite as ruthlessly. Any really recent and expensive cosmetic or cream was spared, but most of the stuff also went. Then the scrubbing and washing: the grout, the shower curtain, the back step, the under eaves on the porch. I moved from there to the recycling. No magazine and no newspaper lived to see the New Year, no exceptions. If it wasn't read by that date, it didn't make it. I got it all out. Finally, I did my clothes. This was the most difficult task, but I usually started this in advance. Everything I hadn't worn in the last year would be given to Goodwill. I continued in this manner to my desk, and by the evening I felt my space—modest though it is—was airy and open to the future. I felt liberated and purged and deeply in control. I have to admit that my rigor was not completely laudable. It existed in tandem and could only exist because of a twinning rigor on the other side of the Santa Monica Mountains. As I did my discarding, my righteous, relentless emptying, Nik was doing the opposite. He was organizing the year's remnants. He was logging and archiving and filing it all. The whole swollen yearlong cumulus. He discarded hardly anything; he wanted souvenirs of every moment. And his accumulations somehow underwrote my eliminations. My liberation was brought to you by the ordered collecting and keeping of my brother. But of course his task was much more complicated than mine. He not only kept, he documented. He annotated, he footnoted, he wrote, he arranged. He updated the Chronicles. (Okay, the Chronicles. Am I already going to digress? Because going into the Chronicles at this point could be a huge digression. But okay.)

By 2004 Nik had thirty-odd volumes of the Chronicles (going back to 1978 officially; unofficially they were retrofitted back to 1973 with the rise of the Demonics). They were all written exclusively by him. They are the history of his music, his bands, his albums, his reviews, his interviews. He made his chronicles—scrapbooks, really—thick, clip-filled things. He wrote under many different aliases, from his fan club president to his nemesis, a critic who started at *Creem* magazine and ended up writing for the *Los Angeles Times,* a man who follows and really hates his work. Nik had given him plenty of ink these past few years.

It is odd to think Nik's Chronicles took some weight off me and my life. I am only tangentially part of the Chronicles. They are truly all about Nik. When I am mentioned, it is largely as part of events invented by Nik. I am only ever in the Chronicles as a figure in Nik's narrative. Like when he produced my girl band back in the early eighties—Hair Krishna. And when I sang backup, or when I happened to be in the house when an interview or photo session happened. It was always entertaining to read what he had me say about his latest record. Or when he had me trying to capitalize on being Nik Worth's sister by launching my own failed TV variety show (which apparently I insisted be called *My Turn.* I thought that was pretty weak and just part of Nik conflating all the women in his life with characters from the *Valley of the Dolls*. I guess I was the Patty Duke character to him, with his projecting on to me a diva-like longing for fame and attention). In the later Chronicles I think I also visited him in one of his stints in rehab (court-ordered), and—oh yes, I testified on his behalf when he was suing his former manager. And one other time when his bandmates all sued one another for divorce. I apparently submitted a friend-of-the-court brief, an unsolicited *amicus curiae.* So the Chronicles were by no means a chronicle of my life. Ada, for instance, was hardly ever mentioned (a few Linda McCartney–style photos of Nik with baby Ada's serious, round face peeking out from under his parka). Nik's Chronicles adhered to the facts and then didn't. When Nik's dog died in real life, his dog died in the Chronicles. But in the Chronicles he got a big funeral and a tribute album. Fans sent thousands of condolence cards. But it wasn't always clear what was conjured. The music for the tribute album for the dog actually exists, as does the cover art for it: a great black-and-white photo of Nik holding his dog with an intricate collage along the edge consisting of images of the Great K9s of History from Toto to Lassie to Rin Tin Tin (credited as "the border collieage compiled by N. Worth"—Nik loved puns, and in the Chronicles all his loves ran without restraint, unfettered and unashamed). But the fan letters didn't exist. In this way Nik chronicled his years in minute but twisted detail. The volumes were all there, a version of nearly every day of the past thirty years.

Perhaps that really is the reason I seem to have such bad recall. Maybe I threw too much out. Maybe I should have kept a few souvenirs. Or maybe I should have been making an accounting of some kind, not just ridding myself of it all so quickly.

So the day started as an unremarkable New Year's Day, and I have no doubt I have fused other New Year's Days with 2004, other jars of moldy preserves and other stacks of unread *Vanity*

Fairs. But I do remember the rest of the day, or at least one very specific thing from the rest of the day. It wasn't even anything that happened to me, it was something I saw on the news in the evening. Actually, I first saw the photo and read about it on the internet. Does that count as a memory of mine? I'm afraid so, particularly this past year, when I felt myself an observer of events more than a participant. But that isn't accurate. I was an absorber of events. They seeped into me, and the first indication of this was on the very first day of the year.

I saw a picture of a pale red-haired woman on the front page of a news website I frequently visit. She looked dazed and older, maybe forty, but a rough forty. The headline was "Mother Arrested After Bringing Baby to Bar in Blizzard." I clicked through the link. I had to—her expression was so raw. The story wasn't anything all that unusual, a banal tabloid tale. She brought her two-week-old baby to a bar on New Year's Eve. She got very drunk at the bar and someone called the police, who then took her baby away. But somehow the story opened up to me. I could picture her walking in the cold, the half mile to the bar, the baby in her baby carrier under her parka. She wants to drink, it is New Year's Eve, she is just starting to feel like a person after the birth. She takes her baby out into the bitter snowy cold—a half-mile walk with a newborn. How unthinkable. But maybe she knows she's a drunk, and she imagines she is being prudent by walking instead of driving to the bar. Maybe she believes she is even being responsible. Or she simply had no ride, no car, no booze. She just pretended to herself she was getting some fresh air. She told herself the walk would be soothing to the baby, that it would be good for them both to get fresh air. And maybe she just "found" herself at her favorite bar and then she stopped in to show off the baby, and she never thought too clearly or directly about how she would proceed to get drunk. Maybe.

I could see her at the bar, cradling her baby against her chest with one arm, lifting her glass with the other. (The short article said "she held the baby in her arms as she drank, alarming some of the customers.") This is what kills me: as she proceeded to get drunk, she was no doubt feeling buzzed and cheerful at first. The bartender and others in the bar coo over her baby. Perhaps someone even buys her a drink to congratulate her. She is feeling high and enjoying the attention. She clutches the baby, who is sleeping, and downs another drink. Then she goes further. I can see her, red hair falling in her face as she starts to talk too fast, too loud. She slurs her words slightly, she doesn't notice the discomfort on the faces of the others. She sways a bit, she has a hazy smile, her face ruddy and her breath sour gin. This is what gets me: she doesn't realize the room is turning against her. She has become this terrifying, appalling display, and she thinks something else is happening. Her misapprehension, then the exact moment she might sense the disconnect. She is now stumbling, and the baby's woken up, and she says she's got to go home and she's got to feed her baby. Some concerned person calls 911. The article also said the woman was breastfeeding the baby when the police arrived at the scene. I can't help picturing that, the baby crying, the woman drunkenly breastfeeding to soothe the hungry kid, the baby rejecting the clumsy nipple and the off milk, the long walk home in the cold waiting for them, and the entire room witnessing her fiasco. And then the cops come and rescue the child. And the mother can barely walk. A tiny piece of broken-human shame.

A little story like that can make me crazy. It just breaks me down. I've never done anything as egregious as this woman, but I can so easily imagine that I am the woman. Something about the need for company, the inadequate mothering, the total collapse of self-protection and dignity. I clicked on the photo and enlarged it so I could study her face. I felt my own face getting red and I could feel the choke building in my throat. I searched her name and found another article at another tabloid site. This one had the same photo of the woman—the only photo ever of this woman, forever. But it wasn't just her—the poor cop who had to take the kid, the poor bartender who served her and then felt queasy as he watched her, the people who sat next to her in the bar—but mostly the woman herself with her pale, bony face and long red hair. And yes, of course I felt sorry for the baby, but everyone feels sorry for the baby. I'm sorry for all those compromised adults, bloodshot and guilty and telling the story later to their friends, just not quite honest about what role they each played in its unfolding.

I'm only at the end of the first day of the year and I am already exhausted and defeated.

JANUARY 2, 2004

Nothing, I remember nothing about this day.

JANUARY 3, 2004

Nothing at all.

The Chronicles never have any blanks. Ever. Nik would've inserted photos here, all flattering. Or a fanzine questionnaire, like this one from his prehistoric teenage Chronicles of the seventies:

I'M WITH THE BAND
The Back Page Vital Stats
Nik Worth tells us his fervid faves and frustrations
Name: Nik Worth
Real name: Nikolas Theodore Kranis
DOB: May 25, 1954, Hollywood, California
Hair color: black
Eye color: brown
Fave song: "Wear Your Love Like Heaven"
Musical influences: SELF. Okay, here: Bowie, Bee Gees, Donovan (see above), J. Lennon, Faces, John Cage, Velvets & Lou, Macca sans Wings, the Residents, Can, John Fahey, Miles, Incredible String Band, Otis Redding, Carl Stalling, La Monte Young, Eno
Pastime: taking walks with my dog Martha

Marital status: single (!!)
Things you look for in a girl: quick smile, patience, love of music, patience, hygiene, patience, pretty hands, patience, trust fund, patience, good sense of humor!
Food: yes [Nik won't admit it, but he has a weakness for sweets. In an interview with another, unnamed mag (*Melody Maker*), Nik once mentioned how he loves Mars bars. His fans then sent thousands of Mars bars to his studio. More get thrown on stage at every gig. Says Worth, "I appreciate the thought, girls, but please—no more!"]
Gear: my gorgeous old Gretsch, my Goldtop Gibson, and my bike, a '65 Triumph Bonneville
Calendar: Julian, but also Sumerian
Quote to live by: Orbis Non Sufficient (James Bond)
Building: The Bailey Case Study House #21 by Pierre Koenig
Book: Deuteronomy. No, Ecclesiastes.
Biggest frustration: I can't hear infrasound
Monoaural or stereophonic: Quadrasonic

It is easy to fill up the space when you get to make everything up.

FEBRUARY 9

My forty-seventh birthday. Ada called me in the morning from New York. She made me promise to look at her blog. She had posted a photo of us, and it said "happy birthday to my mom," just like that, no caps or anything. Not "happy birthday, mom" but "to my mom" because it was really reportage to some audience beyond me. It wasn't a personal message to me but a public announcement about me. The picture was from the mid-nineties. We clutch each other in front of a homemade birthday cake. I would guess Will took the photo. No doubt he gave it to us to keep, but I was sure I had never seen the photo before. I could see our house, the lemon sofa, the sliding glass doors. She was so young, maybe eleven? I studied the picture posted on Ada's blog and felt a surge of hot tears, which I feel all the time over nothing, then sniffed and made myself some coffee. I was wearing my terry-cloth bathrobe, and I felt lumpy and tired. Matronly, *may-tron-lee,* I said out loud, gleefully trying to fuck with myself, but I knew there was more to what I felt than that. I sipped at my coffee. I kept thinking about posting a comment. I should've posted a comment, but I couldn't. I wouldn't ever post a comment. I knew how, that wasn't it, I just couldn't say something spontaneous and pithy and then have it hang there for all eternity. Those are opposite pulls—eternity and pithy—and if I thought at all about what to say, it was even worse. So I never posted, even though I knew Ada wanted that and expected that. Other people would post. Later I would read "Aww, sweet!" from grl4gravity and "Mom's hot!" from mitymitch, which would actually please me in a pathetic birthday-malaise kind of way, an elegiac feeling of my former beauty getting its due or something equally tiresome and full of self-pity.

I ignored my phone when it rang and then checked my voice mail. Nik wishing me a happy birthday. Later in the day, Jay would call and I would ignore that, too.

I got dressed and drove to my mother's apartment. I promised I would stop by on my way to work so she could wish me a happy birthday. I drank more coffee from an insulated travel mug as I drove. Although she lived only one exit south on the 5, I managed to drive right into a thickening hive of slow-moving vehicles. It was mid-morning and I was clumped behind a freeway accident and riding my brakes. I came to a full stop with my exit in sight, a quarter mile of stopped cars between us. Just leave the car and walk. Wouldn't that feel great? I yawned. I could easily smoke while I was stuck in traffic, but instead decided I would listen to a book. I bought it for myself, for my birthday. Happy birthday to me. It was a self-help book, there is no way around that fact. *MemTech: Using Your Brain's Technology at Full Capacity*, which I bought because Mom couldn't remember anything anymore. I told myself I bought it to help her cope with her lapses.

At first she just misplaced her keys. Her wallet. Her glasses.

Minor things. Then repetitions of stories, then repetitions mid-conversation. She seemed more confused than embarrassed about the lapses. She acquired a static but low level of agitation (even actual hand wringing) that made her seem much more unhappy and distraught than she really was, whatever *really was* means. Then we got a diagnosis and I grew accustomed to the idea that things would not improve and at some point I hoped to grow accustomed to the idea that they would not even maintain.

I hadn't paid attention to the introduction and pressed the back button to start over when the exit ramp finally opened to me.

As soon as I walked into her apartment, she started to insist that I take the boxes of used clothes she had in storage to the Salvation Army.

"And get a receipt for your taxes," she said. I could have just said yes, sure. But I had already taken the stuff weeks ago. And we seemed stuck in replaying this same conversation. It always felt tactless to point out the repetitions, but I did because it felt too condescending not to.

"I did it already, don't worry," I said.

"Did you get the receipt?" She had become focused on receipts and paperwork. Our whole life growing up, I don't remember her saying that word one single time, *receipt*. I doubt she ever itemized her taxes even once. But what do I know about her, really? Maybe she always kept meticulous paperwork when we were growing up and she just protected us from all of it. Maybe this was a hidden side of her always there and now leaking out. I doubted it. Now she was interested in coupons, receipts, bills, instructions, warranties, paper trails of any kind.

She kept things to show me. As she grew anxious, the receipts proved something of a comfort to her, a concrete thing she could hold that wouldn't fade like the things she was constantly trying to recall. She nodded and walked into her bedroom. Then she came back to where I was.

She stood in the center of the living room, brows furrowed, eyes darting back to the doorway she had just passed through as though her thoughts might be right behind her, left there.

"What, Ma?"

"I don't remember why I came in here."

"To talk to me?"

"No!" But it was really more like "No!?"

"To find the receipts?"

"No, there was something else . . ." and she looked worried. How could it not be worrying? It could be anything, even something really crucial, couldn't it?

"It doesn't matter. It will come to you if it was important," I said, which was not at all true. She frowned at me. She didn't enjoy this, and it grew harder all the time. But at a certain point she couldn't be aware of things worsening, because that required remembering how they were yesterday or last week or last month. Maybe she read it off me, off the anxiety in my face.

"Do I look older? It's my birthday, Mama. Today. I'm forty-seven—I'm middle-aged." I loved to tell people I was in middle age. It was so terrifying to me that I was middle-aged, it was so deeply impossible, that I wanted to say it all the time.

"Oh, happy birthday, sweetheart. You look just lovely." She sat next to me on the couch. The blankness and anxiety left her face.

"You and Nicky got to pick your cakes. Do you remember? I had this booklet of fancy-shaped birthday cakes and how to make them? The *Wilton Book of Birthday Cakes.*" She just pulled that title out of some pristine cerebral crevasse.

"Yes! The *Wilton Book of Birthday Cakes,* I totally forgot about that thing. I used to pore over it, plotting my cake months in advance. The Rocketship cake, the Raggedy Ann cake, the Holly Hobby cake."

"They were complex cakes, you had to bake sheet-pan cakes and then make stencils so you could cut them in the right shapes. Then you had to decorate them properly. According to the instructions."

"Yes, that must have been so much work. They were great, we loved them."

"You decided you were too old for funny-shaped birthday cakes, remember? You said that was for babies. But I knew you still wanted a cake, you just couldn't admit it. So I went in your room and I found a picture on your bulletin board—"

"*Aladdin Sane*! Of course! How could I have forgotten that? You made me a beautiful Bowie birthday cake! It was amazing, with the frosting lightning bolt across his face. I forgot all about that. That was amazing!"

We both were so thrilled that she remembered something I had forgotten. She beamed at me, nodding. Then she started to laugh, and she looked like my full, young mother for a moment. She reached for my hand and squeezed it. Her hand felt cool. Her skin looked old, but it felt soft and delicate. It wasn't smooth and fat like a child's skin, but it was almost softer.

"I have to go to work," I said. I could hear my voice quake

and jerk. Usually I was fine when I was with my mother. Usually I didn't start to cry until after I left her, when I was in the car, driving. But there I was, hard-swallowing and sniffing. "I'll be late. Mama, I love you."

"I love you," she said, and we hugged. I didn't let go for an extra second. Pay attention to this. Hug tight, this could be one of the last hugs. I had been making myself think this way since I'd turned forty. My mother was not that old, but she had diabetes. She was overweight. She was not healthy. And even if she didn't die in the next few years, her mind was rapidly slipping away. Maybe one day soon the hug won't be with my mother, but with her body and what remains of her. One day she'll hug me and mistake me for someone else, and so these current, somewhat intact moments were fleeting. I noted that, marked it in my mind. Don't forget what it was like to embrace her, all of her, and don't let it be replaced with what will come, soon, a certainly diminished future, or at least a wholly different future, because, as her doctor said without exactly saying, it will only get worse.

I have always been the sort of person who is easily panicked about how quickly time passes, but in the past this was mostly related to Ada. I would remind myself not to get too distracted, because four would soon be five would soon be ten and then her childhood would be gone forever. I remember frantically looking for the dimples on the backs of her chubby hands, convinced I would be so sad the moment I noted their certain replacement by knuckles. I would kiss those dimples—and as much as I missed them, I loved the beautiful hands that emerged. But this current accounting with my mother was so much darker: she would be less and less and then she would be gone. A memory. Ada became an adult with all of her baby brightness intact, fully realized and elaborated. And I wouldn't have to witness her unwinding and diminishing. That would be her daughter's burden.

But I knew this was not even true. I knew other horrors awaited. I knew that just as I was starting to fall apart right in front of my mother, just as I knew my mother must note my sad middle-aged visage, I knew I would live long enough to see Ada start to grow old. Already when I see her I notice how she looks more tired in tiny ways. I would live to see her get crow's-feet and gray hair and hands that showed veins. I would see her feet and her neck change. I would see the perfection of her body be undone by time. I might live to see her lonely, divorced, unhappy, and a hundred other disappointments. What you don't think about or plan for (as if that helps) is watching your children get old. The privilege of a long life is you live long enough to see your perfect child also submit to time and aging.

So, on my forty-seventh birthday—if that was truly my middle age—what did the second half of my life hold for me? I would watch my mother and her friends and siblings die, one by one, but also all at once, a flurry of funerals, then watch my brother and my friends as they speedily replaced them as failing beings on the way out. Everyone knows that is just how it goes. I'm not the only one, right? And let's not forget I get to experience my own dwindling vitality, which will surely accelerate and reach critical mass in the next fifteen years.

I stood in my mother's doorway and scanned the room. Soon she would have to move from this apartment—it went in-home aide to assisted living to a full-care facility to a hospice. I was just waiting for the thing to reach the next level. Whenever I visited, I was vigilant in looking for signs of new deterioration. Was she wearing pajamas in the afternoon? Did she smell clean? I expected to find rotten food in the refrigerator, a carton of old milk congealing in the cupboard. But her routine—and I made sure it was always the same for her—could stay intact for the moment. I checked in with her most mornings, and her home health aide came in the afternoon to help her with dinner. Once a week we went shopping and had lunch together. She appeared to hold at this point, but I couldn't stay where she was—I waited and watched for what came next.

I think on some level I always imagined Nik would never make it into old age, how could he? He didn't make those kinds of mistakes. I knew he would die of cigarettes and drinking long before I would finally die. I just got to witness and witness and stupidly survive. The second half of my life was just the bill due for the pleasures of the first half. And Nik would get to escape payment.

I left her apartment, sniffling and congested with my little birthday pirouettes around mortality. A fitting birthday disposition, but then I began to fixate on how I had managed to forget that birthday cake. I realized I couldn't actually locate it in my memory. I could remember only the photograph we took of the cake. Not the feel of the pink-and-white frosting in my mouth, not the gulp of cold milk I no doubt drank after a few bites. Oh sure, I could conjure a sweet cake-taste memory, but that was a generic substitute, a little made-up game. All that remains is a photo of that cake, somewhere, in some album. It does not help, having a photo. I believe—I know—that photos have destroyed our memories. Every time we take a photograph, we forget to embed things in our minds, in our actual brain cells. The taking of the photograph gets us off the hook, in a way, from trying to remember. I'll take a photo so I can remember this moment. But what you are really doing is leaving it out of your brain's jurisdiction and relying on Polaroids, Kodak paper, little disintegrating squares glued in albums. Easily lost or neglected in a box in your waterlogged garage. Or you bury it in some huge digital file, waiting to be clicked open. All you have done is postponed the looking, and so the actual engaging, until all you are left with is this second-generation memory, a memory of an event that is truly only a memory of a photograph of the event. It is not a real, deep memory. It is a fake, fleeting one, and your mind can't even tell the difference.

These very ordinary memory failings gathered weight and had grown into a quiet but desperate obsession over the last few months. I started to take note of them right after we finally got my mother's official diagnosis.

The official diagnosis:

Her doctor said she had age-related cognitive decline, also called mild cognitive impairment, very common for a person in her seventies, and that this was no longer called senility, which really just means oldness. Eventually it would probably become mild dementia and then full-blown dementia, which is a kind of scary-sounding word that simply means the mind is going away. So you have to specify age-related dementia instead of, say, drug-induced dementia. My mother exhibited significant early symptoms of age-related dementia including but not limited to advancing episodic memory impairment and disorientation. Very commonplace, he said, which was supposed to be a comfort. When pressed, he also remarked that her decline was most certainly progressive. But everything was progressive, clearly. Did we actually think our memory had any stasis? That it wasn't constantly melting away?

After that, I began to find her troubling to be around for all the obvious, emotional reasons. But I also had a growing worry that her lapses were somehow contagious. I had no rational basis for this anxiety—clearly her brain was distinct from my own brain. I also knew I was probably avoiding a more frightening mortal anxiety by substituting a slightly more manageable one. But.

The traffic was gone now. I still had a forty-five-minute commute to work. I didn't have the heart to listen to the memory book, the self-help book. I pretended I had bought the stupid book to help my mother, but I knew I was really buying it to appease my paranoia about my own mental deterioration. Maybe just owning it would be enough and I wouldn't actually have to listen to it.

Then, out of nowhere, randomly, I had a memory crisis, a mental meltdown over a seemingly insignificant piece of information that I tried to recall. I don't know what led me to try and retrieve this particular piece of trivia (because I don't remember!), but there I was, floundering as I drove, sweating even, chewing hard on a herbal, soon-to-be-flavorless piece of gum. This sort of memory slip was all too typical of my brain these days.

Sometimes basic words of familiar vocabulary hid behind missing letters. I would run through the alphabet, hoping I would get the right sound by process of elimination. More often, a name I knew refused to come to me. I constantly had the sense of information on the verge, precision at the margin, vision just beyond the frame. Not like Mom, not not remembering what I was trying to remember, this was not remembering what I sort of nearly recalled. It was like a glitch, like a scratch on a record. I even hit my head occasionally to get the needle to jump to the next place. I knew, somehow, moving forward was often the best way to remember what came before. Looking at a thing directly didn't work. I also knew trying so hard just caused surges of stress-induced cortisol to shut down my hippocampus, sealing off access to my long-term memory. Still.

This time I was trying to think of a movie actress's name. I came up with Mamie Van Doren. And I knew that was not who I was trying to think of. I was trying to think of another blond actress, one much more famous than Mamie Van Doren. I thought about her, this actress with the out-of-reach name, and how she was decapitated in a tragic Cadillac accident. I thought of her famous custom-made heart-shaped swimming pool. Yes, anyone would have it now, but not me. Marilyn Monroe was at the other end of the bombshell spectrum, this actress was ersatz Marilyn, and Mamie Van Doren was ersatz her, ersatz ———. I saw her face, her little nose, her chalky pink lips, her enormous breasts. (Enormous in the old way, fleshy mounds that attached to the whole chest, Anita Ekberg oceanic flesh that might drown a man, instead of the modern-style augmented, separate, too-high globes with the huge lonely valley between them, carved breasts that seem to exist almost in a different world from the body they are attached to. But how could I assess the pertinent advantages of real versus fake enormous breasts? Maybe men like that hard valley, maybe they like the delineated order of the implanted, artificial breast.) I could not think of her name.

My mother would get that vague, anxious look as she realized she was searching for something that wasn't there, and then she would forget it, the forgetting, and move on. She just let things go without a fight, and then she was on to the next thing waiting to be forgotten. I could not let go. I started to talk out loud, I shouted, *What the hell is her name?* sending the now flavorless gum flying out of my mouth. I retrieved the gum with a tissue as I tried not to swerve the car. And then I began to recite the outlines of the memory as if I were pleading a case to the dementia police—I can't be losing my memory because I can think of Mamie Van Doren, I can think of the breasts of this poor unnamed actress, I can think of her method of death, for God's sake, I can think of a stupid movie she was in with Tom Ewell. I can think of Tom Ewell. I have, clearly, an excellent memory, it was merely a glitch. Then I tried to do some lateral move, to think of something else. But really, moving on when you were more or less still assigning a portion of your brain to this elusive memory task, it fooled no one. Ada would say, *Just look it up, Mom.* But that was easy for her and her young, elastic, fearless brain. I wouldn't, I wouldn't look it up on the Internet Movie Database or Wikipedia or anywhere else.

Ada doesn't understand why I need to remember every random piece of nonsense—it is almost as if she believes the internet will be her memory. I want to warn her: I've been through this with photographs, it just isn't the same as actually remembering. I see her point about cluttering your brain with easily looked-up trivia, but there are other things I need to remember. Things not found on Wikipedia. I want to remember my mother before she was sick. I want to remember what Ada smelled like when she was a baby, and I want to remember when I began to suspect things weren't okay with Nik. I want some accounting for my own behavior, and I want the future to have some clarity. I need my memory for all of that to occur. That is why incidents like this one were so critical. If I couldn't think, on my own, of this actress's name, I had no hope for any of the rest of it. So I used Calm Focus (memory technique #5). I inhaled and exhaled. I was so close, I felt it, it was almost there. It was like a brain orgasm, the anticipatory sensation I was feeling, a kind of building. Then I got Anna Nicole Smith, and I couldn't stop thinking of her hard little eyes and her little doll nose and the same chalky pink lipstick, but it wasn't Anna Nicole Smith, of course, and now I was stuck again, the closeness receding. I had a name, Mamie Van Doren, and a face, the pudgy pretty face of Anna Nicole Smith, but I was further than ever from my actress. In fact I had to keep pushing these other people off my mind. The only way out of this very frustrating trap was to look it up. Defeat, yes, but peace. I took another deep breath. Damn it. Okay, one last recap: Tom Ewell. Cadillac, decapitated. Pool, lips, breasts. Then I saw it, the book with the black-and-white photos, yes, the picture of her and her breasts, yes, closer, yes, no Mamie, no Marilyn, no Anna, no, but Man, yes, yes, Man, Icouldevenseethecoveredstretcherinthephotoas shewastakenfromthesceneof—

Jayne Mansfield! Jayne Mansfield! Jayne goddamn Mansfield!! Yes, yes. Yes.

So there, happy birthday, it was in there somewhere, all of it. Memory of a photo of a woman and, indexed in synapses and dendrites, a name.

FEBRUARY 10

The day after birthday night. I spent the evening with my sort-of boyfriend, Jay. He came by after I got home from work, bringing take-out food and a movie. After we ate, he handed me a box neatly wrapped in red paper.

"Gee, what can it be, I wonder?" I said, as I knew what was coming. I unwrapped the package. It was a Thomas Kinkade Painter of Light$_{TM}$ Lamplight Brooke Music Box. The music box was in the shape of a vaguely nineteenth-century streetlamp. A transparent snowy night scene aglow with a sickening preternatually golden light lined the inside of the glass lamp. I laughed—it was impossible not to.

"It's hideous, wow," I said.

"Wait, play the music," Jay said. I turned it over and wound the key. The music started, and the snowy scene was further illuminated from a bulb within. The music, I realized, was "What the World Needs Now." Of course. This music lamp was not the first Kinkade item Jay had given me. We had been seeing each other only a few months, and I think he had already given me six Kinkade pieces: the Thomas Kinkade Painter of Light$_{TM}$ Hideaway Coffee Mugs (Hideaway being one of the collections—it referred, apparently, to the fatly pastoral cottage engraved into the porcelain), the Thomas Kinkade Painter of Light$_{TM}$ Holiday Lights Animal Holiday Village, the Thomas Kinkade Painter of Light$_{TM}$ Lighthouse Light, several limited-edition picture plates, and one print "painting," also limited edition, that featured golden highlights actually painted on the print (not, I would guess, by Thomas Kinkade Painter of Light$_{TM}$ himself, but by little indentured gnomes and elves). Jay gave me the first one about a week after our first date. He just gave me the package with no explanation. I unwrapped it and opened the box to reveal this deeply hideous object. He didn't laugh at all. He pointed out the Certificate of Authenticity. For some reason I loved it. I don't even particularly like kitschy stuff. Having grown up in a dilapidated house in Hollywood, I liked actual solidly beautiful things. But Jay taught art history at Wake School, an ultra-elite private arts high school in Westwood. And Jay was British. So somehow he became obsessed with Kinkade. When I asked him why Thomas Kinkade, he just said, "Well, he is America's most successful artist. And a native Californian as well." Or he would say, "His name has a trademark—see?" and he would point to the subscript that appeared after his name. He was a brand, Thomas Kinkade Painter of Light$_{TM}$. And I remembered how Nik would always carefully draw his copyright symbol on the hand-made labels of his records. Whatever publishing company name he had for that group and that record would never fail to have that rights-designation insignia. Jay's arbitrary fixation amused me, and his focus and repetition impressed me. Even the stupidest joke can become funny with enough pointed repetition. Even the most pointless obsession can yield a certain kind of depth if it is pursued unfailingly. Jay was unrelenting in his obsession.

He didn't veer off subject and suddenly start collecting Ronald Reagan Lobby Cards or vintage Mammy Salt Shakers or mint-in-box Dawn Dolls. He brought only Thomas Kinkade Painter of Light$_{TM}$, and it wasn't entirely a joke, he really was fascinated by these objects. It actually isn't arbitrary, is it, a true obsession, although it may appear that way to an outsider. It may even be mysterious to the obsessed person why something grips him so, and that mystery must feed the obsession, increase the profound hold. (Ask someone who is truly obsessed *why* they feel that way. They will sputter, they will feel you are interrogating their private world, they may spout a list of reasons, but ultimately they can't fully explain it. Obsession has an irrational or subrational heart. It is a bit like falling in love, I imagine.) And I believe few things are as despicable and dishonest as faking an obsession. The world is full of the lightly obsessed, the faintly committed, the inch-deep dilettantes. All those contrived and affected and presented passions. Jay was authentic; Jay had depth.

I am drawn to obsessives. I'm not one myself, so I can only guess about this stuff—okay, maybe I have obsessions, but mine are useless, neurotic obsessions. I am talking about aesthetic-driven, artistic obsessives. I sure am surrounded by them: Jay, Nik, even Ada in her way.

Jay slept over, which he did now once every week or so. It had become a regular thing, not increasing or decreasing in intensity or frequency. It held. We had slow, easy sex that had a low-volume erotic tone. We weren't in love—even the idea of that made us both skittish and nervous—but the physical pleasure was real and steady and welcome.

Knowing I would see Jay once a week also helped me keep

some minimum level of grooming: I shaved my legs, I did my nails, and nearly regularly did my pilates DVD. I first met him at the Farmers Market on Fairfax, which is near where I work as a secretary for Greer Properties. I mean office manager. I mean personal assistant.

It was at Du-par's, an old coffee shop where I eat lunch a couple of times a week. I used to occasionally see Jay there, reading. One day, on my way out, he asked if he could have lunch with me the following day. Jay wasn't a good-looking guy. He was in his mid-fifties, balding, and he wore sweaters that were too big for him and created an off-putting, almost creepy diminutive effect. Nevertheless, he did have a faded British accent. I said yes.

We agreed to meet at the same place. As soon as I sat down with him, I regretted it. The whole thing felt so awkward, and now this coffee shop would be forever poisoned with failure. I'd have to eat somewhere else. We ordered and then sat in forced smiles and silence. I became very conscious of how often I seemed to blink. I drank too much coffee and then I began to talk, and talk, filling the empty air.

"Have you been following the severe acute respiratory syndrome global pandemic? You know, SARS? Well, you remember how at the beginning of the year it was constantly in the news? Every time you turned on the news they were talking about it. All winter long we heard about where it was and what could be causing it. We saw people in hospital beds on respirators next to photos of them healthy and smiling at a barbecue. Interviews with family members and CDC officials. Remember? Well, then SARS just stopped for no reason.

Do you know there were over seven thousand cases?" I said, leaning in.

Jay nodded politely. I believe I mentioned "corona virus" and "etology" and "case-fatality ratios" and I didn't stop. I hadn't been out with a guy in a long time, but even I knew talking about infectious diseases was not appealing first-date conversation. I finally took a breath and he looked uncomfortable.

"What do you do?" I asked, my whole person collapsing in weary resignation as I asked this ridiculously boring question. This was exactly why I stopped dating. This was why I wanted to stay with my husband long after I realized he was unhappy. So I wouldn't have to ask and answer these sorts of questions.

"I'm a teacher," he said.

"Oh, that's great. What do you teach?" I said. To me, asking and answering these questions implied a false promise about the future. Telling your life history meant you were throwing it out for someone's perusal, and how optimistic could you feel? How could anyone "get" me at this point? I made no sense, especially in light recitation.

"I teach art history. And sometimes film. At Wake School. Do you know it?"

I shook my head.

"It's a private high school for rich industry kids. Mostly. They do give some financial-need scholarships to gifted kids."

It was my turn, and I found myself speedily talking about Ada and her life in New York. And I knew I now sounded like a woman who lived through her daughter, but I guessed that was better than the woman I was a minute earlier who loved to talk about SARS. I was just about to launch into describing my dying mother and her approaching dementia and my own fears of age-related memory impairment when I stopped. I just stopped myself. I took a sip of water, a deep breath, and I let the silence hang there. I even stopped smiling.

At last he said, "You have the loveliest hands," and he put his hand, or just the fingers of his hand, very gently on top of the fingers of my hand. I could feel my cheeks getting warm. I stared stupidly at our hands on the table. At last I looked up, and he was looking right back at me. I made myself hold his gaze for a second, and I could feel an unmistakable wave of desire move through my hand and across my body. I had to shift a bit in my seat, even, and I was amazed at how a man who didn't seem sexy at all could suddenly become starkly erotic just by plainly admitting his desire. Was it always like that? I didn't think so. I think it had a lot to do with the many pointless bad dates I had after my second husband, Will, left me (I refer to him as my second husband, but I never actually married Ada's father, Chris, so Will is in fact my one and only husband, or he was before he left me). I went through setups and contrived dinner parties and even an online dating service. How difficult and humiliating it was to discover a man wasn't really attracted to you. There was a time when a man's attraction was a given, and that time had passed. I stopped trying to date after barely a year. It had, I'm afraid, been a long time. Sitting there, with his hand on mine, staring me into desiring him, felt good—quietly, dizzily good.

I would have liked to do something then, but. "I have to go back to work," I said. I gently pulled my hand back toward me. He let go.

"What work do you do?"

"I'm a personal secretary. Or assistant. An office manager for Greer Properties. A sort of personal assistant to Jack Greer." The Greer family had real estate holdings all over Los Angeles. They owned land from pre-Hollywood time, orange-grove time. They were even related to Henry Gaylord Wilshire on his mother's side. Wilshire used to own property from West Hollywood down to what would become Wilshire Boulevard, which he planned to develop from a barren field into a grand street named after himself. He donated the property to the city in the 1890s. Henry Gaylord Wilshire frequently ran for office as a socialist and eventually lost everything; Jack's money came from his father's unsocialist grandfather, Lymon Greer.

I have been working for Jack Greer for fifteen years. I do everything for him, from making lunch dates to getting his dry cleaning. I answer letters and return phone calls. I distill the important request from the nuisance or the extraneous and then deliver it to the attention of Jack. But mostly I just have a long-built instinct for what he wants to hear about. I do, however, have to be there without fail, to filter and distill. No spontaneous late lunches for me.

Jay smiled and nodded. Not that interested in hearing more, which was fine because I wasn't all that interested, either.

He came over for dinner that night. It would be a long drive for him. I lived across the Valley and way into the tired desert hills of Santa Clarita. He lived near the Farmers Market, on Ogden Drive. Already we were doomed, we had a commute between us. But he didn't complain, and arrived on time. He did not bring me a Thomas Kinkade Painter of Light™ item that evening. That would be saved for our next date. We ate grilled fish with aioli and drank a steely and unsentimental summer wine. We talked about Nicholas Ray's hard-to-see film *Bigger Than Life,* in which high school teacher James Mason takes the newfangled cure-all drug cortisone and then becomes sweaty and distorted and psychotic. He loves Nicholas Ray and I love James Mason, so we found common ground in *Bigger Than Life.* Because it hadn't made it to DVD, it had attained a cult cachet among film fanatics. Jay—no surprise there—was a devoted cineaste, particularly of the highly wrought American films of the 1950s. Jay emerged from his car proudly wielding an old copy of the film on videotape, which I thought was a rather interesting date choice. Though no fanatic, I had seen *Bigger Than Life* at the Nuart years ago. Whatever it was to people in the fifties, or to the film fanatics of the moment, to me it read like a very earnest description of middle-class mortal desperation. It didn't feel silly or campy, despite how melodramatic I found it. It truly disturbed me. It was a much more discomforting film of addiction than, say, *The Man with the Golden Arm.* It was about the creeping perversity of conventional life; it was, with its increasingly distorted close-ups and subjective angles, its blatant angry reds and hysterical atmospherics, a deeply unsettling film.

We tapped it into my old VCR. This time I didn't feel disturbed. Instead I felt as if an old friend had dropped by. I now loved this odd obscure movie.

"Did you ever think about how men in the movies are rarely shown as high school teachers? How they are always university professors? I think we are supposed to think Mason is a failure because he teaches high school," Jay said.

"What about *To Sir with Love*? That was a male high school teacher. He was the hero," I said.

"That was a redemption drama—a missionary film. Totally different."

He poured out the rest of the wine. Mason was in his bathroom, popping pills with an anguished expression.

"Don't look in the mirror! Whatever you do, don't look in the mirror! Oh, he looked in the mirror," I said. I was pleased to make Jay laugh. It is nice when you have seen a movie a few times and you have someone you can talk to while you are watching it. The repetition makes the movie lose some of its darker impact, but it gains something else: as it seeps deeper into familiarity, it begins to make a permanent claim on your sensibility, your aesthetic history. It is a lens through which you see the world, and that requires a certain amount of interaction, of movie talk. And I love that. I hate when people say *shhh, shhh,* like you are in church. I want to watch a good movie again and again, and again, and I want to crawl into it with my friends and talk. Jay didn't *shhh* at me. Not at all.

"It is hard to buy Mason moonlighting as a cabdriver. It seems so unlikely to me. He does do that seethy humiliation and self-loathing so well, though," I said.

"Did you ever notice how in all his movies James Mason always has a scene in a robe? In *Lolita,* in *Five Fingers,* in *A Star Is Born.* And in *The Seventh Veil.* Mason, it appears, was required to wear a robe in every movie he did," Jay said.

"Not in every one. Not in *The Desert Fox.*"

"Yes in *The Desert Fox.*"

"He didn't wear a robe in *The Desert Fox,* did he? A Nazi smoking jacket?"

"I'm afraid he did. A rather smart dressing gown, with a matching monogrammed handkerchief pressed to his mouth from time to time. Don't you remember how they have to drag him from his convalescent bed because he is the only one who really understands the desert?"

"I never actually saw it," I said. "But you're on to something here, he has these robe scenes, doesn't he? A very neatly tied robe. Or perhaps a smoking jacket. Maybe it is because women want to imagine him in these intimate circumstances, but they also want to imagine he is stern and elegant all the time. Robert Mitchum or Burt Lancaster, they could be sloppily bare-chested. But if we saw James Mason in careless naked abandon, it would be like the end of civilization."

"Except *Age of Consent.* I recall a growling Mason rolling around naked with Helen Mirren in *Age of Consent,*" Jay said. "Of course, that was the sixties—"

"Oh my," I said. "That's just—"

"Yes," Jay said.

After the movie, we had a gentle, tentative kiss. I took his hand and led him to my bedroom. We undressed in the forgiving twilight. He was slight, with mottled middle-aged skin, standing naked by my bed. A little like James Mason, I thought, with his accent and all.

The next time we met, he brought a copy of *The Seventh Veil.* I hadn't seen this film before. It not only starred a young and severe James Mason with a mysterious Byronesque limp, but it also featured a woman with a memory problem pulling back the "veils" to recover her troubled, fragmented past. It was hard not to like a guy who had an instinct for indulging my eccentric longings.

Jay and I began to meet once every couple of weeks. It was an affair without urgency or agenda, it seemed. We'd see a movie—he continued to bring me hard-to-see films—we would have dinner, and we would sleep together. In the morning we would say goodbye. But we were not in love. We didn't have those exhausting conversations that in-love people have. We didn't talk about our failed marriages, although I did discover, eventually, that he was once married to an American woman. We didn't do the life-story stuff. I knew only what pertained to the present—that, for example, he would be gone for two weeks around the holidays so he could visit his family in England.

After he gave me my birthday present, we watched *Odd Man Out.* I didn't tell Jay any of my birthday anxieties. Not because I wanted to withhold something. I just didn't feel them when I was with him. I didn't want to talk about myself; I wanted to talk about movies. Somehow, in the time between being young and where I was, the life-story recital grew too long, both dull and complicated. When I was eighteen, I wanted to tell my lovers every inch of every moment that led to this miraculous moment. I thought that would make them understand me, and then they would have to love me. But now that I was older, and actually had a life story, I didn't feel like telling it or hearing it. I just wanted him to press against me as we slowly figured our bodies out. I understood our real stories lived there anyway.

FEBRUARY 14–15

Ada came to visit. My favorite thing is spending the occasional weekend with Ada. When she still lived in LA, she would come over for dinner every week or so. But now that she lived in New York, I would get these wonderful weekends with her. I would take a plane to the city. I would stay with her in her studio apartment in Greenpoint. She would introduce me to her latest boyfriend. We would go have a glass of wine at her new favorite bar. We would sit up late talking. Even after we went to bed (in her double bed, under her pale pink satin duvet with the large, pale pink Art Deco swirls of stitching and cording), we would continue talking. What did we talk about? She told me everything. And I listened. We were like college girlfriends.

This time she was coming to LA for two nights. She had a documentary film project she was trying to raise money for. Her production partner, Lisa, had set up some meetings at the cable channels that supported beginning filmmakers. We sat on the patio and ate cheese and drank her favorite rosé champagne. Her early years of waitering in nice restaurants had left her with expensive tastes in food and wine. I delighted in pleasing her and strove to spoil her for the few weekends I had with her.

"I drove over to Nik's today," she said.

"I invited him to come by tonight, but he didn't feel like it."

"He is so funny—he showed me his latest Chronicle entries and played the corresponding music for me."

"I'm sure he loved doing that."

Ada took a sip of her pink wine. She took a drag off her cigarette. I know this is an awful thing to say about your kid, but she looked good with a cigarette. I thought this, even knowing how my brother fell into long hawking fits every morning. And coughing fits throughout the day. Bronchitis every winter. But when a young person smokes, it is different. It just underlines their excess life. It looks appealing and reminds you they feel as if they have life to spare. They have such luxury of time that they can flirt with lethal addictions. They have plenty of time to heal and repair later. A young woman like Ada would eventually discard these things. When you are old, like Nik, when it is a very old habit, smoking looks mostly like a reckless delusion. But for Ada it was an abundance, a kind of fun, a kick off of a shoe, a sip of pink champagne.

By any standard, reasonable light, I appeared to be a crappy mother. I had an inappropriately casual relationship with my daughter. Of course her father, Chris, saw it that way. Even Nik—*Nik,* for God's sake, the least judgmental person on earth—thought I was too easy on Ada. It is all true. But Ada, somehow, still managed to become this wonderful, thoughtful young woman.

"I think I want to make a movie about Nik," she said. "You know, he really is like a folk-art genius. Not just his music but the whole deal, the whole constructed lifelong thingy. He would totally be a great subject. Don't you think?"

I thought about it. Nik might be a good subject. He was so eccentric, so hardworking, so unapologetic. But I didn't think enough about it, or about what making a movie would do to the delicate balance of a secret life. I forgot, maybe because it was Ada, that I needed to look out for Nik.

"He would be a great subject, and he would love it. But then again, he might not be totally receptive. Nik, he seems like he's hungry for attention, but I'm not sure he is. Not anymore. Besides, he is used to controlling the whole story."

Ada glanced at me and nodded. She had short, shiny black bangs and long, straight black hair. Her eyes were heavily lined and the penciled-in arches of her brows precise. Her eyes looked enormous, even as (or because) her lids appeared halfway closed when she looked straight at you, sleepy kewpie-doll eyes.

I poured myself more champagne. "We might have to talk him into it. Nik has his world, and I don't think he even sees himself . . . Let's put it this way: I think his whole life is a private joke that he doesn't want to explain to anyone." I took a sip of champagne and felt the bubbles fizz on the sides of my tongue as I swallowed. "And I think part of his pleasure, or at least his freedom, is he doesn't think anyone will see it or judge it."

Ada nibbled at a cracker with a delicate sliver of cheddar on it. She had the eating habits of the relentlessly waifish.

"I don't know. Of course, it's up to him—he will know if he wants to do it."

Ada nodded.

"But what if people think the music isn't any good?" I said, something I never considered before because it just didn't apply. I listened, I paid attention, I enjoyed.

Ada straightened up and leaned across the table toward me. "You think his music is, uh, not good?"

"I do not think his music is not good, or what we sometimes call bad. I think, with as much certainty as I can bring to these kind of judgments, that Nik's music is really, really good." I had never said that in quite that way before. It took on more certainty as I heard myself say the words.

"Me, too. It's great. Totally great, c'mon," Ada said.

"And we are so objective, aren't we?" I said. I started to laugh, and then I felt sad about laughing. I didn't need to throw up all these cynical equivocations any time I said something important. Not even equivocations, but little sarcastic tics. It didn't feel good, or even particularly true. We sat there without talking for a few moments. The lights started to come up from all the houses in the surrounding hills. When I first moved to Santa Clarita, the hills behind my house were empty. I used to be able to hear coyotes howling at night. I wasn't supposed to feel this way, but I didn't entirely mind all the development—at night, seeing the lights of the houses reassured me.

"I think Rob is seeing someone else," Ada said. "No, seriously."

"Of course he is. He's *married,*" I said.

"No, I mean someone else, not his wife, not me."

I sighed. (I actually made some of those mouth-clicking or sucking sounds, usually written as a *tsk* or a *tut,* but that doesn't look right to me.) I liked Rob. I had never met him and probably never would meet him. But from what Ada had told me, he was very funny and smart. He didn't lie to her. This was clearly another instance of my poor parental guidance. I know

I should have disapproved, but she appeared to be so in love, so happy. Ada's father, I was sure, had no idea of the existence of Rob. Only I got to be her trustworthy confidante.

Ada started to cry.

"Oh, honey, come on."

Ada sniffed, then she smiled and wiped under her eyes with her knuckle, pushing back mascara and tears. "I'm okay," she said. I put an arm across the back of her shoulders and squeezed her toward me a little. It was more of a buck-up gesture than an actual hug. She would be fine.

But I should have realized how the movie would complicate things.

FEBRUARY 17 AND 18

Nik called to tell me his old bandmate Tommy Skate was dead. Congestive heart failure, which was expected.

Nik had made me come with him to visit Tommy a few months ago. I hadn't seen Tommy in years. He was the original lead guitar player in the Demonics. He used to wear plaid pants and creeper shoes with a wifebeater T-shirt. Tommy smoked menthol Marlboros because they made his breath smell good. He asked me out about fifty times from 1977 to 1990. Tommy played in punk bands, new wave bands, power pop bands, grunge bands, and so on, then he stopped playing. Later he became a Buddhist (he still indulged his every desire, but he would lecture you about "letting things go"), he developed a leather fetish, he defended Ronald Reagan, and he knew everything about martial arts movies. He worked lots of bad jobs, but mostly I remember he worked at a hospital switchboard, because he would tell stories about the crazy calls he would get at three a.m. Oh, and I guess Tommy was married once to a woman I never met and then quickly divorced. He never had any kids.

Tommy moved back in with his mother when he got sick. They shared a two-bedroom house in the Valley. It was an aging 1950s ranch, with sunflower wallpaper in the kitchen and mossy wall-to-wall carpeting in the living room. We found Tommy encamped on the sectional couch near a large TV.

Nik hadn't said a word the whole ride over. He drove, smoking and holding the wheel with one hand. The CD playing on his stereo was one of his own productions—I never understood how someone could listen to his own CDs. Isn't that just unimaginable, or at least indicative of a malignant solipsism? But Nik, going back a long while, listened to his own music if he listened to anything. The older he got, the less he wanted to hear any music at all. It seemed to irk him or bore him, but less so when it was one of his albums. I can imagine no equivalence to this in my own life—again, we have veered so far from each other. Except I also listened to Nik's music, so we had that in common.

An ancient air conditioner hummed overchilled but under-circulated air into Tommy's house. A stale sweet smell barely covered the acrid and unmistakable yellow stink of a lifetime of cigarettes. I didn't ever tell Nik how much it bothered me, that same sad undersmell in his apartment—he was used to it, after all. Tommy sat with his feet up on a pillow. His ankles and feet looked swollen to the point of formal uselessness. His wrists and fingers appeared puffy and immobile. He explained he could no longer play his guitar, but he still could play the keyboard. He explained further—just the sound of those words, *pulmonary edema,* whispered our future to us. *Myopathy, necrosis, infarction*—the serious words I would put into search engines late at night and then watch them multiply.

Tommy turned the knob on his old stereo until Richard Hell and the Voidoids poured out of the speakers in the high-volume requirement of both 1978 punk rock and damaged old ears. Hell's sneery vocal instantly grated on me. At first I thought Tommy chose it for the horrible ironic effect of punk vitality. But then, as I watched his hands weakly chug along to the contrary guitar, I could see that Tommy really loved the noise, the refusal and the stubborn assault of it. It wasn't an ironic gesture, it was a sad and nostalgic gesture.

"I hate this album," Nik said.

"Yeah, but the guitars," Tommy said.

"The guitars," Nik said, a concession lurking in a nod and pursed lips. Nik wore his sunglasses, but from where I sat at his side, I could see him dart glances at the room, at Tommy's swollen white feet, at the array of pills on the side table.

Tommy's face—his nose in particular—had grown doughy over the years. I tried my best to conjure how he used to look in the old days. Without moving my head, my eyes looked up and back, as if that would somehow help me see the past better. Maybe people do that with their eyes because looking at the present is too distracting. I could glimpse him standing at Nik's bar maybe fifteen years back. It was horrible to contemplate how much the past fifteen years had worn on him, or, really, on all of us. He was truly unrecognizable, just a damp, congested distortion of his younger face.

I didn't say anything to Tommy as we sat there, I just listened—how could I not, at this volume?—to the music. We all felt relief when the "hit" came on, "Blank Generation."

I belong to the blank generation and
I can take it or leave it each time

The nihilism of the lyrics came with a bright up-hop to the guitar riff and some nice sloppy *ooh*s that made us all feel momentarily happier, though it couldn't have been lost on any of us how young the music sounded, how ridiculous.

"It's just the—" Tommy started, then paused. We looked at him. "Shit, I can't get the word I was about to say. It is the strangest sensation, knowing something but not being able to remember it. How can you not remember it if you know you forgot it, you know?"

"It's called aphasia. That sensation—you remember the thing but not the word," I said. "Nominal aphasia is when you can't recall names." They stared at me. "I have it, too, all the time."

"Oh, fuck, everyone gets that," Nik said. Although Nik had an excellent memory for an unrepentant alcoholic. He never forgot anything.

"It doesn't matter," Tommy said, but I could tell he was still trying to think of it. Nik took out his gifts: his latest CD in a Collector's Limited Edition case and a liter bottle of handsome-looking scotch.

"I figure if you can't drink much, it should be the best, right?" Nik said.

"Thanks, man." Tommy looked at it. "I can't drink at all anymore, it interferes with all these meds. I can't tolerate it at all. But it sure is nice to look at the bottle. You want a shot?"

I was so irritated by this. I just hated, deeply, the idea of Nik taking a shot. Right here, in front of bloated Tommy, in the morning. And I hated that Nik spent a lot of money on an expensive bottle of scotch when he had no money. And then, through my anger, I figured it out—he knew that Tommy couldn't drink. He knew that he would end up drinking it himself.

Nik uncorked the top and poured some in a water glass. He threw back his head and slammed it down.

"Is that the way you're supposed to drink that kind of scotch?" I shouted over the music, and I heard the pointless harsh scold in my weary rhetorical inflection. They didn't even look at me, and who was I to rain my judgment on them, now, after all? This was a special occasion; I was a prig. Except there would be another shot, surely, and another, and then we would drive home, me terrified not that Nik would crash—he seemed unaffected by drink—but that he would be pulled over and get a DUI. Which wouldn't be his first. And maybe he would lose his license and then wouldn't be able to get to work. At the very least it risked a big fine, not to mention the possible bench warrant that was no doubt outstanding from previously unpaid tickets. Fifteen years ago Nik actually had to spend a couple of weeks in jail. All due to years of ignored traffic tickets. He stamped handcuffs in the LA County Jail. And washed police cars. They let him leave the jail to sleep, I think. I don't remember. He was pretty careful for a while after that, to pay or respond to tickets. He had become more careless the last couple of years. Careless or reckless? None of this appeared to concern Nik in the slightest as he downed another shot. Tommy dissolved into a hacking coughing fit, and then we watched as he worked to find his breath.

As soon as we left Tommy's door, Nik felt in the pocket of his jacket for a cigarette. In the walk down the driveway, he lit up and took a deep drag. He would chain-smoke all the way home.

I knew Tommy upset Nik, and I knew that the scotch and the cigarettes calmed him down. I knew that. I also knew that he had coughing fits similar to Tommy's. I had never bothered to ask Nik to quit smoking. Not once. I knew he never would. I had asked him about other things, drink and drugs, at various crisis points. He would not consider my concerns, my calculations, my projections in fear and the future. He would say, more or less, *This is how I want to live and I won't complain when it finally takes me out.* Which was true, he did not complain. He wouldn't curtail his life to protect against some theoretical consequence that might never come to pass. Unlike most normal people, he didn't regret his habits and he never even pretended he would try to quit any of it.

By now I should have been used to his—what should I call it? Need? Requirement? Accommodation, maybe? He wouldn't call it an addiction. He would call it his consolation. As far back as I can remember, Nik always used—the consoling part came later—whatever was at hand whenever he could. He just wanted and needed to get off his face, out of his head, expand, shut down, alter, spin, fly, sleep, wake up, float. When we were small kids, we would grab each other's arms and swing in circles faster and faster until our brains' equilibrium was nauseatingly off. We would walk in staggers and feel the earth come up to meet us in giant waves as we collapsed in breathless laughter. This odd feeling was a pleasure, and enjoying it is common, right? Nik also loved to wind the chains of a swing in creaking twists, pushing his leg off the support poles until the chains would twist to their very top, then he would push himself in the opposite direction, flying in tight fast circles as the chains unwound, throwing his head back to augment the spin. I read somewhere that the brain needs disorientation to properly develop. That childhood desire to feel dizzy has something to do with increasing the vestibular and cerebellar interaction in the young brain. Proprioception is the activity where the brain orients the inside world with the outside world. Spinning throws off your proprioception and the brain works and develops as it tries to get it back. The desire to spin around is healthy, I guess, because it teaches the brain how to get a stable fix on the world under any circumstances. But Nik got stuck there, somehow, and had to do these activities over and over. Getting dizzy-high was just the beginning. Swing sets were his gateway drug. Nik had an intense appetite, a special extra need, and as he grew older he grew more hungry for any and all alterations. I watched it; it was impossible to miss his difference, how he craved anything that undid his equilibrium.

He began drinking coffee in third grade. He would make it with instant coffee crystals and lots of sugar. He would mix it cold with tap water. He often stayed up all night (which is another childish and cheap way to get high—stay up all night and the fatigue alone will make you feel giddy). He drank OTC medicine, all kinds: decongestant to get speeded up, cough syrup to sleep. I swear he always smoked cigarettes, but of course that can't be true, he started at maybe twelve. By junior high he was taking any drugs he could get his hands on, and he could get his hands on so many.

Like the most serious druggies, he lived by the PDR, the *Physician's Desk Reference,* the well-thumbed paperback book that made his drug experimentations seem so rational and considered. He would root through his girlfriends' mothers' medicine cabinets. He would take a few of these, a few of those. The PDR would tell him what the drug would do, what the pill looked like, and it would tell him what it would interact with. He knew what he could mix or not mix. Nik became the guy you asked, *How many should I take?* Nik was the guy who helped the kid who turned blue or the girl throwing up in the bathroom at the party. And his gleeful hunger to alter his brain never abated and was never apologized for. In his youth he extolled theories of the need and even obligation to get high. He quoted the usual hallucinogenic pantheon of Huxley and so on. He didn't miss any rationales for his enthusiasms: Huichol Indian peyote, Freud's cocaine, Leary's LSD, Richard Harris's scotch.

As others of us (me, for instance) grew bored taking drugs, of "experimenting," he never stopped. He wasn't experimenting. But as he lived longer and longer into his aging, creaking habits, he stopped trying to extol them to everyone, or at least to me. If it came up at all between us, it was usually because I decided I wanted him to change his habits out of simple health or plain decency, or even economy (the cigarettes I never mentioned were now five dollars a pack). He would simply tell me that this was his consolation. And what could a sister say to answer that?

On the drive home from Tommy's house, we didn't say anything to each other until he idled his car in my driveway. Before I got out, he said, "Thanks for coming with me."

"It's real bad," I said. He nodded. I climbed out and then I leaned into the open window to kiss him goodbye.

"At least it can't get much worse," he said with a broad smile. "It really can't."

Three months later, Tommy finally died. The day after Nik called me about Tommy, I opened my mail and found a copy of the obituary Nik had composed for his Chronicles:

New York Times, February 18, 2004

Tommy Skate, 49, Dies;
Guitarist for the Demonics

Tommy (Skate) Lester, the original guitarist for seminal garage rock band the Demonics, was found dead at his home in Van Nuys, California, on February 16, 2004.

Dr. Sam Wills of the Los Angeles County Coroner's Office certified that the cause of death was heart failure. Dr. Wills said no autopsy would be performed. Lester had a long history of drug abuse and alcoholism.

"The Demonics came out of nowhere to totally transform the 1979 scene in LA, working a unique sound counter to both commercial progressive rock and punk rock," said Robert Hilburn, music critic for the *Los Angeles Times.* Lester played on the Demonics' first two albums: 1979's *Waiting for the Game* and 1980's *Sound Fantastique.* Despite its dark lyrics and art-rock dissonance, *Sound Fantastique*'s fatal hooks and crafted melodies made it one of the best-selling records of 1980 as well as one of the most critically acclaimed. Nic Worth, lead singer and songwriter for the Demonics, remarked once that "Tommy Skate's undulating leads really gave the Demonics their unique, intense sound." A legendary band that broke up even before their second record was released, their influence long outlived their brief years together. The oft-repeated rock'n'roll cliché about them is that although the Demonics didn't play very many shows, every person who did see them live seemed to have formed a band of their own.

Thomas Lester was born in 1954 in Los Angeles. His father worked for the postal service and his mother taught piano. His mother bought Lester his first guitar for his 8th birthday. He attended Fairfax High School, where he met the other members of what would later become the Demonics. His first group was the short-lived proto-glam band Sticky Baby, which had a sixteen-year-old Nik Worth as lead singer. They played a simple heavy blues boogie in semi-drag that was later taken up by other bands as "raunch" rock. When Worth and Lester quit Sticky Baby to form the Demonics, they vowed to abandon blues-based rock forever.

After the glory of the Demonics, Tommy Skate was in a number of much less interesting and successful bands. He embraced a harder, faster, and more generic style; he abandoned his eccentric edge (against the advisement of his mentor, Nik Worth) for what he thought was a more commercial sound and eventually he stopped playing in bands altogether. The money he made from publishing royalties from the songs he coauthored on the Demonics' records helped support him over the lean years, but throughout the eighties and nineties he also worked periodically in fisheries in Alaska, at a hospital, as a gravedigger, and as a garbageman.

He is survived by his mother, Glenda Lester, and his brother, Jim Lester, both of Los Angeles.*

**Correction 2/19/2004:*

The obituary for Tommy Skate on February 18 misidentified

the high school where the band the Demonics was founded. The Demonics were started at Hollywood High School by Nik Worth, not Fairfax High School. Only after Worth transferred to Fairfax High School did Tommy Skate join the already formed Demonics.

Nik couldn't help getting his licks in, but he still nailed the odd tone of the rock and roll obituary, the way it would leaven even the most sordid life with comforting obitual formality. I knew this because I was a regular reader of obituaries. Before I read anything else, I scanned the obituaries. I wasn't always like this, it was a habit of my morbid middle years. I just found myself drawn to them every day. Why? I don't think it is hard to guess. I first looked for the age of the dead person. If they were under sixty, I looked at the cause of death, usually discreetly rendered in the second or third paragraph. (Nik's obit for Tommy was less discreet than was typical; usually the drug use isn't mentioned but just screams between the lines of the rock star found dead of "heart failure.") Very young people mostly die in accidents. Most have not lived long enough to accomplish anything notable, and they rarely get full obituaries. So the saddest obituaries are the premature but not uncommon middle-aged "young" people, say between thirty-five and fifty. These folks do indeed die and I always took note:

47, ovarian cancer
53, heart failure
58, complications from pneumonia
54, breast cancer
46, self-inflicted gunshot

59, pancreatic cancer

38, motorcycle accident

48, breast cancer

58, overdose ("yet to be determined," "toxicology report," and "bottles of various prescription medications")

35, drowning

46, died in a fall

57, sudden heart attack

50, heart attack suspected

42, heart and kidney failure

45, car accident

59, complications from a brain hemorrhage

49, killed himself by hanging

59, lung cancer

40, sudden cardiac failure

50, ovarian cancer

I think that anyone would get the picture here. No peaceful, natural deaths. It was either bad luck or bad living. Or, I guess, a bad attitude (the suicides).

FEBRUARY 20

Nik sent me his latest CD. I found the package in my mailbox (he always mailed his CDs to me). I undid the undecorated, restrained brown paper packaging. *The Ontology of Worth: Volume 2,* it said on the spine of the CD jewel case. Volume two of twenty volumes. But he counted backward, so the next album would be the first—and presumably the last—volume in this epic series. *The O.O.W.* was released on his experimental record label, Pause Collective. He began it in the mid-nineties. Every six to twelve months he would release an album in the series. Each CD had an edition number. Mine was number two, which meant after Nik's copy, I got the very next one. Always it worked this way. There was a handful of fans (let's be clear here: with the exception of Ada and me, everyone was either an ex-girlfriend or an ex-bandmate) on the mailing list, but I was always number two.

Not only did each disc have a limited edition (10? 12?) handmade cover, but each cover fit into a larger piece. This CD cover would fit, I knew, with the eighteen previous CDs in the series to make a huge self-portrait collage of Nik. Each cover worked on its own but also played a part in a larger mosaic. Just to have the second-to-last piece felt like a long battle almost won—were we really coming so close to completing the epic, endless thing, or would he extend the plan? I didn't see how he could get out of the finite rubric he had created.

In addition to the CD, there would be a vinyl release (which would just be the 12-by-12 cover with an old dummy piece of vinyl in it—he didn't actually have the ability to press vinyl). But the paper center label would be carefully covered with one of Nik's hand-painted adhesive labels. His Pause Collective was strictly for wackier, non-pop experiments. Its elaborate center label featured a color photocopy of a pen-and-ink snake carefully drawn in hundreds of hatched lines with a distinctly occult/medieval feel. The "logo" contained the word *Pause* hidden in the complicated hatches of the snake. The name of the album, the copyright date, the catalog number, and the name of the artist (uh, Nik Worth) were inked on top of the photocopy in a careful, matched script of Nik's devising. The back of the LP usually had liner notes. These would be written on the cardboard in the same font. A photocopy, or sometimes a typed copy, of the notes would be pasted carefully in the Chronicles. And another copy of the liner notes would be folded up and tucked next to the CD in the digital edition, as well as reproduced in a photocopied and barely readable size on the back of the CD case itself. It was all quite systematic and gratuitously laborious. I loved its elaboration and counted on it. How deflated I would feel if he ever just handed me a blank paper sleeve containing only a blank compact disc with his name and the title Sharpie-scrawled across it. (Nik did make some faux bootlegs that had a cultivated amateur feel to them, but he never had the taste for the sloppy or the minimal. Even his bootlegs appeared to be made by obsessive fans with acute horror vacui.)

I unfolded and read the liner notes for *The Ontology of Worth: Volume 2:*

When I first met Nik Worth back in 1978, he was in two bands and not yet a star. He fronted the power pop band the Fakes. They would have three songs in the top ten by 1980. And back then I already guessed it. There were the clean, perfectly rendered songs of heartache and youth. The crystalline gorgeous harmonies got them compared to the Beatles. But they were also minimal in production, they never overwhelmed the songs with sentiment and bombast. They had a pared-down, solid unadorned sound. They resisted the ubiquitous processing of the time. (Remember gated reverb? Have you listened to any of those records lately?) They bucked the trends, the boilerplate, and yet—or maybe I should say, and so—attained top-seller status. That would have been career enough for anyone. But, as we also know, Worth also fronted the Demonics, and anyone familiar with their two brilliant albums knows that Worth was already testing boundaries and breaking new ground.

When he broke up the band in the early eighties, he embarked on a marvelous, unprecedented path of experiment and innovation. He would release a brilliant Fakes album every year, each one charting and succeeding. But he also nurtured a new path leading to his releasing two solo records under his own name, Nik Worth. These were made on a four-track in the living room of his isolated estate in the hills of Topanga, Western Lights. He was holed up for months, and rumors of a car accident or a drug habit multiplied. The truth was, Worth had gone through a nasty divorce from model

Alize Clement. During the divorce proceedings, he was driving his vintage Triumph motorcycle on the PCH and crashed. No one knows the full details of the accident, but he retreated to his private hermitage in the mountains to recover. Part of his recovery included the recording of these ache-and-angst solo records. The critics praised the new direction. Both of the albums have cult followings, but neither of them charted.

Then there was nothing for four years. Until 1990, no releases from Worth except the Fakes' album HERE ARE YOUR FAKES, *a double album of previous hits and some unreleased songs from the vault. It was the top-charting album of 1989, and fans scoured it for clues about the future of Nik Worth and the Fakes. Nik Worth, we later learned, had been living as a Buddhist monk in a monastery in New Mexico. He took a vow of seclusion and adopted the Dharma name Jikan, which means "silence." Would he ever record again? In 1990, we got our answer. Worth got the old lineup of the Fakes back together and recorded an all-new studio album,* TAKE ME HOME AND MAKE ME FAKE IT. *It is generally considered to be the sine qua non of nineties power pop albums. Then, in 1992, Nik Worth also released an album called* THE ONTOLOGY OF WORTH: VOLUME 20, *on his own mysterious label, Sound Traces (later to become Pause Collective). This album was apparently the first of twenty planned releases starting with twenty and counting backwards to one. As soon as you dropped the stylus, you were hit with the central thematic conceit of the Ontology: side one contained six bled-together linked songs about a character called Man Mose. The entire side two, infamously, contained one "song," a cacophony of feedback experiments that were somehow tied to the story of Man Mose. Full of cryptic and hermetic references, Man Mose (one gathers) lives in tunnels under the streets and hears things through the ground as he moves from place to place. He apparently makes or records his "music" all the time. Side two is the music MM hears (makes?). Underground music, indeed. Who would have guessed that what we were all waiting for was a collection of atonal, arrhythmic assault compositions mixed with concept sound poems?*

Undeterred by a rather chilly reception, Worth would go on to produce eighteen more of these albums over the next twenty years, each more "underground" than the last.

What have we learned about Worth from this long journey of slow baroque noise, garage concrete music, Indonesian gamelan evocations, electronics, acoustic low-fi living room experiments, trance and Ramayana monkey chants, sound collages, narrative and anti-narrative, soundtracks for unmade films, dissonance and odd slack-key guitar tunings, Komoso ametric and polymetric music, tape loops and audiotape manipulations, dub and sampling, prepared guitar and piano modifications, silence and his so-called "sounded silence"? And always in there somewhere, however faintly, Man Mose appearing and disappearing like the trope that refused to die? Does the willfully obscure and difficult music play against and in effect count on the need to make order of it, to make it cogent, what Karl Popper described as "the intrinsic and constant drive to find congruence"?

*Critics have called it "naive and embarrassing" (*Village Voice, *1992). The Ontology has also been called "the most pretentious work of any rock star, anywhere, ever" (*New Musical Express, *1995). And about Ontology: Volume 3: "A painful illustration of the limits of autodidacticism" (*Rolling Stone, *2001). But to those of us who stuck with it, there has been an undeniable power* *in these accumulations. If approached with an open mind and an open heart (and perhaps some mind-expanding hallucinogens), and if approached with a willingness to dwell in the endless run-out groove of another's obsession, these albums can lead you on a riveting journey. Is* VOLUME *2, in fact, the penultimate record? Is this epic, eccentric freak ride coming to an end? Listen and judge for yourself. As Worth has said, "It's all there, it's all there."*

Mickey Murray
Greil Marcus Professor of Underground, Alternative, and Unloved Music
The New School for Social Research

I slipped the CD in my purse to listen to on my drive to work. I sat at my computer and went, as I always do, straightaway to Ada's blog. I saw that she, too, had received Nik's CD:

lowercase a:
daily musings of an unemployed but brilliant filmmaker
February 20
As my loyal readers know, nearly every day I run from the West Village to the river. Today's run stood out from the others. Yes, that's right, I got a new record from my eccentric uncle Nik. (For those of you late to the lowercase a *party, you can read what I have posted about him* *here* *and* *here* *and* *here.) As I ran through the sliver of the west side park, always in sight of the Hudson, my ipod was loaded with my uncle's new release,* The Ontology of Worth, Volume 2. *Those of you who frequent this space know how much I dig my intense uncle's complicated self-published recording career. And you might also know his experimental stuff is not my favorite, especially*

his epic (ahem) experimental stuff. I prefer the pop stuff, the side projects, the low-fi simple songs. He can make perfect three-minute pop songs that will hypnotize you and haunt your every waking second. But the epic dirge pretensions of the multivolume work? No thanks. The avant-garde (I guess, but avant-garde circa 1975) noise/song cycles, the hermetic codes and references, the doom and the darkness that seem to deepen with each volume. Not my style, way too ponderous and concentrated for me. It's at best annoying and at worst unsettling (maybe that's the other way around). But, as I am your ever-open-minded lowercase a, I touched play. No music on this at first, just spoken words. "Soundings," he calls it. I gave up guessing (but so much about the fun of music is that kind of guessing at what is coming and then being surprised or disappointed, being satisfied or being bored). I let the "Soundings" wash over me as I hit the rhythm of the run. I went with it. And wow, I must tell you, it blew me away. It was the perfect mix of the moment and the sound. And it also gave me an idea. Stay tuned and I'll tell you what it is!

a.

I hadn't had a listen yet, and I felt a pang of regret reading Ada's "review." Often Nik would review his own records for the Chronicles. He had several rock-journalist pseudonyms that he used when he wrote these reviews. Many, of course, were hyperbolic raves. Some were carefully considered and annotated essays that were in fact fascinating exegeses by the artist. And quite a few were scathing, harsh hatchet jobs or faint, lethal dismissals. Nik would sometimes send me copies of the reviews with the CD. I would make a point of not reading them until after I had a clear, unframed listen of my own. In this case, there was a "clipping" included, but it was an interview from Nik's fantasy fanzine, *Butter Your Toast*:

BUTTER YOUR TOAST

Our Girl Anna Conda Tracks Down the Elusive Nik Worth

Western Lights, Topanga Canyon, California

Today, fans, is the day. *Volume 2* of *The Ontology of Worth* has hit the stores. Looks like we are getting very near the end! Don't miss it, or the free promo poster, and don't forget the limited-edition covers all work together to make three different unique images (back copies are still available for the previous eighteen volumes, but hurry—they are limited and are already commanding high prices on eBay). We have been informed that once these discs are gone, no more will be made!

Nik Worth, aka Nikki Trust, né Nikolas Kranis, pop wunderkind turned underground wizard, has agreed to talk to us about his latest release:

Butter Your Toast: What made you decide not to use music on some of these tracks?

Nik Worth: Why not? I like to experiment. Call it a Futurist sound experiment, a dada poemlet.

BYT: Yeah, okay, but when are we going to get some pop songs?

Nik Worth: The Pause Collective is not a pop label.

BYT: How do you expect your fans to listen to this?

Nik Worth: I expect complete and total attention for all of my work. I want my fans to drop whatever else is going on and devote themselves. I want them to listen, with rapt and dire attention, to the prior eighteen volumes, in order, and then I want them on their knees, eyes closed, with the whole fifty-six minutes of the CD played at top volume. I want them to repeat that undistracted deep listening until they see the patterns, themes, and ideas that link and resonate through the entire nineteen volumes. I want them to understand any failings they may perceive in the work as part of its terrible beauty, and I want them to embrace the mystery and beauty of the project as a whole. Then I want them to hold those thoughts and feelings and wait breathlessly for the final chapter—*Volume 1*. Soon to come. That's all I expect.

BYT: And when will you drop the final chapter, *Volume 1*?

Nik Worth: Sooner than you think. This year. I'm almost done.

BYT: And?

Nik Worth: It cannot, I repeat, cannot, be topped. This truly will be the last record.

I know. There was no mistaking the finality of his statements. But to be fair, I had heard things along these lines for years.

FEBRUARY 21

I do all my listening in my car. It is the only thing that makes my commute bearable. Each day I get up earlier to "beat" traffic. I had begun to leave my house while it was still dark. I watched the light gradually press behind the mountains; the glow of the headlights of the few other cars made me feel as if I were part of a secret, determined club of commuters. I inserted Nik's CD and tapped up the volume button to a nearly uncomfortably loud level. I wanted to feel the music as well as hear it. In the anticipatory silent seconds before any sound could be heard, I felt a little lift of desire and possibility, something that felt marginally like wanting a cigarette or a morning coffee or, more aptly perhaps, starting the last chapter of a book you have been reading for a long time. I had a second to wonder, breathlessly, what world would come. This little edge of wondering right before was an active part of the pleasure: the matrix of expectation based on the past, the thrill of the unknown that isn't fully unknown because the work is from such a familiar, intimate source. I knew, in a larger sense, what was likely to come. I, after all, had heard so many of Nik's CDs—each and every one of his CDs, which was no small amount—all of his CDs, as far as I could tell. And listened closely, listened with devotion and attention. It should be somewhat predictable by now, shouldn't it?

Nik's voice came on. He spoke instead of singing, and there wasn't any music.

A spoken-word intro? Really? But then I stopped. I listened. I knew how to listen to him. He had earned that unique faith that comes from knowing the work and the person making the work. He wasn't reciting words, but rather rhythmic sounds. Wordish sounds. They were nonsense but compelling somehow. He chopped a sound and let it hang there, unrushed. I felt a movement forward, a lean in me toward a future second. I picked up the CD case. My left hand gripped the top of the steering wheel. I glanced at the thickening traffic on southbound 170, made a minor calculation that I made so often: a person in control of a speeding car (seventy miles per at the moment) could momentarily not look at the road she traveled but could sneak a look at a piece of writing, or at the radio controls or a telephone keypad, and the risk that something would happen that would require her eyes and attention—well, it was worth taking, as it was unlikely to have any consequences given the brevity of these glances. The CD said: *"Track One: Soundings (32:10)."*

Well, okay, Nik had his pretensions, and I was also glad to know that it just didn't matter. Just as it didn't matter if he was repetitive or derivative. It also didn't matter if he was stuck in some dead-ended wrong-turn rut where experimental music met art met folk met acoustic rock and roll. (Did that rut even exist? Maybe briefly back in 1979 or so—I was, of course, making all of this up, guessing, more or less. I had no idea of the precursors and probably neither did he, but even if he did, it would not stop him. Nothing would ever stop him.) Nik was liberated from any dialogue with the past work of others and certainly with the current work of others. His work was his own exclusive interest now and had been for years. I knew his solipsism had become his work, in a sense, that this was complicated to think about, but at some point there is the unyielding, the concentration, and the accumulation that becomes a body of work. Whatever the nature of that work, it is hard to argue against. Maybe. I'm not sure about it. In this case, Nik's case, it meant he could do whatever he wanted. No one—not me, certainly—could deny that this was a form of purity.

SOMETIME IN MARCH

How could I have missed how things had begun to escalate? He had developed a swollen foot, which made standing difficult for him. I determined it was a kind of rheumatoid arthritis—what they used to call gout. I came by to bring him some prescription-strength anti-inflammatory pills that my doctor prescribed for what he used to call premenstrual syndrome but now depressingly calls perimenopause syndrome. Nik had called me, complaining of a tremendous pain in his toe. I dismissed him at first, but it soon became clear he really was in terrible pain. He didn't have insurance, of course, how could he? And he felt too stupid to go to the emergency room over a sore toe.

I got off the phone and went straight to work. I made my diagnosis through the internet. I spent several hours (it was never less than that when I tried to figure these sorts of things out) online. I typed symptoms into search engines (inflamed toe highly painful) and then tried to evaluate the vast responses such searches returned. I would "refine" my search and try again, as instructed. Eventually I reached a stasis, a sameness and repetition factor, that would lead me to a hypothesis. I figured that if enough people said it (wrote it) in enough places, that had to mean something. I thought it was gout. I plugged *gout* in to Wikipedia. Here is what I found:

> **Gout** (old name: **podagra**) is a form of arthritis caused by the accumulation of uric acid crystals (due to hyperuricemia) in joints. It is an immensely painful disease, which in most cases affects only one joint, most commonly the big toe. Patients with longstanding hyperuricemia can have *tophi* (uric acid stones) in other organs, e.g. the cartilage of the ear.
>
> Historically known as the "The Disease of Kings"[2] or "Rich man's disease."[3]

I also found the Wikipedia boilerplate medical disclaimer:

> **Wikipedia** contains articles on many medical topics; however **no warranty whatsoever** is made that any of the articles are accurate. There is absolutely no assurance that any statement contained in an article touching on medical matters is true, correct or precise.

I was, out of necessity, less rigorous than Wikipedia. I concluded that the prescription-strength nonsteroidal anti-inflammatory, coupled with Preparation H liberally applied to the swollen toe, would offer Nik some relief.

I stopped by Nik's house, his "hermitage," aka Western Lights in the Chronicles, which in actual life is an eight-hundred-square-foot apartment over a dilapidated garage studio. I liked the last part of the long drive from my house to Nik's apartment: up and over the winding Calabasas pass to get to the secluded and forgotten corner of Topanga Canyon where he had lived the last twenty-odd years. The best thing about the place was it was set back from the road, hidden behind several gnarled canyon oaks and clumps of shrubby manzanitas. Nik had divided the upper space into two large rooms by building a wood screen. One was the bedroom. The other was the living room/kitchen. One wall offered mottled light through a row of prefab aluminum-framed sliding windows that were characteristic of the flimsy warm-weather structures built in the fifties and sixties, back when Topanga was still a rustic, bohemian paradise full of artists and disaffected underground movie actors. The edge of the yellow-and-brown vinyl linoleum kitchen floor had up curled at the threshold join to the main room, so it caught your shoe and tripped you when you walked through; the Formica counter was cracked and peeling; and the kitchen ceiling had radiating cycles of ancient water-damage stains. But it was not dirty—Nik always kept things clean and in working order. The double garage underneath was given over to Nik's use, so he had room for his recording studio and for storage. Nik spent most of his time down in his garage/studio or at his worktable. The upstairs rooms underlined how the rest of his life (eating, sleeping, fucking) had become increasingly rudimentary. He had never been single for more than a month until these last few years. His last (known to me) girlfriend was Alize. Alize was okay, I guess. She was a washy blonde, very thin, very aloof. After their first inseparable year of lap-sitting and private jokes and finishing each other's sentences and cigarettes, they didn't get along at all. They continued on and off for several more years; she kept turning up so much I thought she might last forever. But two years ago she finally got married to someone else, and I wasn't sure, but I was pretty sure, that they no longer saw each other. (Alize was still on the short list of people who got CDs. She was number three, I believe.) I never got very close to Alize. She was forever trying to enlist me in emotional manipulations of my brother, trying to get him to "get real." Which was really funny coming from anyone who knew Nik at all. She once suggested we do an intervention, a cruel and crude ganging up on someone by every known and trusted intimate in his life. I refused.

"This is a person, if there ever was a person, who will not change. I promise you, what you have is all you will ever get," I told her. But she knew that. We all knew that. It was just very hard to take, his obsessive work habits that yielded (what felt like) willful esoterica combined with his truly unsustainable consumption habits. Accepting a person like that in the long term is hard even for a sister, but beyond hard for a lover. Especially as Nik got older, the real issue, I think, although no one will admit it, became Nik's lack of resources. He lived with no financial future, a middle-aged dive-bar worker with no ambition about money. Few women could accept that. I used to dream he would meet a very rich artsy widow who would fall in love with him and his work. She would sponsor and keep him. I remember even counting on it as a real possibility—for many years his wide-set gray eyes and his angular hollows made him a prodigious male beauty (albeit the oddball/bizarro type)—but the rich benefactress never appeared. Not even close.

The door was open when I arrived. I found him lying on the couch in sweaty, red-faced pain. I could smell that Nik had been drinking (to alleviate the pain, of course). He couldn't put a sock on and certainly not a shoe.

"You gotta go to the doctor."

He laughed.

"What?"

"I'm really broke right now. I've already missed a week of work." I nodded. I tried to put the Preparation H on the swollen sausage toe. He yelped. I gave up.

"Maybe you should go to the emergency room," I said. "They won't make you pay. I can take you over there." He shook off this suggestion. He took a sip from a glass filled to the brim with a caramel-colored liquid and a few melting ice cubes. As he swallowed, he closed his eyes and took a sharp breath in.

"You know, drinking really makes it worse."

He nodded, as if to say, *No doubt.*

"But especially beer. You can give up beer, can't you? Don't make me tell you about tophi and what unleashed urates eventually will do." And I also knew, but did not mention, that this gouty arthritis could often develop in tandem with much more serious illnesses, this feature being sweetly termed *comorbidity*. Not wanting to alarm him, I did not mention the list of possibilities delivered to me via the flowing and all-leveling directionless coursing of my online research. But the huge amounts of repetitive medical data, the folk guesses stacked next to scholarly papers, the self-help encyclopedias by the pay-per-access medical advising sites, the automatic diagnostic tools that led to the badly designed sales sites of holistic treatments—all of it—were not directionless, actually. They all led back to you and your lonely, sad little search. Each decision you made, each click or go-back button, each time you put one more thing in the search box or bookmarked a page, this was your desperate, pathetic self applying some insular logic and order to the information, however inadequate it might be. It exhausted you because you got lost in the flow of endless data, and it exhausted you because you never stopped trying to find your way in it, to apply some little spit of personal agency to it. It was a fucking war, that's what it was.

He placed two of the shiny white liver-toxic NSAID pills I brought him in his mouth and washed them down with a swallow of bourbon.

"That will make you feel better."

He paused, put a hand to his mouth as if he were holding down something vile, then swallowed and nodded.

Denise put down her pen and clasped her hands as she stretched her arms up toward the ceiling. She shook her head and yawned. Two p.m. She should call someone. She ought to make some phone calls. She went to Nik's bathroom and washed her face. She considered using Nik's toothbrush, which he had left, and instead just gargled with green Scope.

She called her mother and told her she wasn't coming today, but not to worry, the home aide would be there soon. Denise also called her boss. She heard herself say "sick." And that was it. No police, no Ada, not yet. She just wanted more time. She walked back to the desk covered with the papers she had been filling. She wasn't ready to stop.

She picked up an open pack of cigarettes that sat waiting on the edge of the desk, right within reach. She picked up Nik's Zippo and lit one up.

The tobacco smoke curled into the room. She reached for the bottle of Evan Williams and poured some bourbon into the glass on the desk. It was all rather pleasant, rather comforting to her. She hadn't eaten or slept at all, and now she felt it instantly as she swallowed a long warming pull, puckery and sweet. The bourbon and the cigarette smoke together. She could almost smell her brother.

She plucked a new pencil from the jar of neatly sharpened pencils. The chair was padded and she could adjust it up. He had it all figured out, didn't he? The little world inside the big world. The world within the world.

But here is what she did not do: She did not put on his clothes. She did not play his guitar. She did not brush her hair out of her eyes in his manner. She did not imagine she had become her brother. She did not indulge in some rigged transmogrification like in that weird Roman Polanski movie. She forgot the name of it. *The Tenant*. She did put out her cigarette after only a few drags. That was enough. Ridiculous. Denise laughed out into the room. She took another sharp sip of the bourbon.

She took *The Ontology of Worth: Volume 1,* out of her purse and put it in the CD player, easily reached from her present perch. She hit PLAY. She heard his voice, and then she clicked it off.

She was going about this all wrong—sequential, linear, chronological. From day to day. There were other ways, other connections that were maybe deeper, other ways of ordering and contemplating and telling and showing.

~~MY FRAGILE BORDER MOMENTS~~
BREAKING EVENTS

Confession.

If I am honest. If I can be truly honest. Memory doesn't reside in dates.

Memory resides in what you notice, what you feel, what catches in your mind. And the things I remember best about the last year are not conversations with Ada or dates with Jay or helping Nik. All of those things fuzz into one another. The things I do remember best are not my experiences at all. They are what I call the permeable moments: the events that breached the borders of my person. Let's call them breaking events. I don't mean breaking news. I mean breaking of boundaries. These are incidents that penetrated my mind, leaked the outside inside.

Okay. Ever since my mother got ill, or ever since I began to suspect things were not right with my brother, or ever since Ada moved away to New York, or just ever since, I can't quite negotiate the border between myself and the world around me. I am not referring to mere empathy or generosity or expansiveness. For example: when, on New Year's Day, I read on the website I visit on a daily basis about the woman arrested in the bar, I didn't have the normal person's indifference. I got caught up. I got obsessed. I ruminated, I investigated. I developed an unhealthy correlative feeling of suffering. I developed a nearly debilitating sympathy, sometimes for the least sympathetic among us.

Okay. I watch a tremendous amount of television, mostly cable news. Further, I spend hours on the internet. And I read the newspapers. There are many hyped and excessively covered news events. Most just mildly engaged me, but some really got to me and overwhelmed me. I didn't have the proper defenses any longer.

SARS was maybe the inaugural incident. My outsize preoccupation and concern about SARS was fairly ordinary contemporary hysteria, nothing that standard narcissistic hypochondria and paranoia wouldn't yield when mixed with the right amount of overblown media yelping. But things soon moved to a different level, a deeper, more personal level. And it wasn't just the big things—little, barely covered things got to me. Like when I noticed this newspaper photo of a middle-aged, heavily built man. He was in an orange jumpsuit and those awful manacles they put on the wrists and ankles of prison inmates. His face showed no emotion, but if you looked closely, you could see the wet streaks on his cheeks where tears had streamed down. I became instantly tearful myself; as I read about him, my tears grew to sobs. After twenty-seven years of prison, he was being released because DNA evidence had finally exonerated him. His stoic expression belied by tears, his suffering, I felt it, but also the misery of a life lived every day of those twenty-seven years, the things he thought or did to console himself, the injustice he had to live with every day—how could I not be moved? But I couldn't stop. I wept and wept. I cut out the picture. I read everything I could about the details of his case and his life. I was inconsolable. I never cried like that for anything that happened in my actual life. That is my problem. This is what I am getting at. My vivid memories of these seemingly random news events. And my fuzzy, fading memories of my actual life.

How can these invasive, overwhelming external events be called my memories? I do partly remember by news cycle. I'm quite serious. *It happened after the anthrax scare but before Daniel Pearl was assassinated.* (Not just important cultural touchstones either. As in *It happened right around the time Laci Peterson disappeared.*) This is the thing, the shame: my memory is dominated by events external to my actual life. These events, for whatever reason, stick in my mind and become secondhand memories. Although I did not experience the events, watching them and reading about them and my reaction to them was a kind of an experience nevertheless. It sounds so meager when I describe it, because the feeling it finally recalls really is, no matter how intense, meager.

It reminded me of watching a certain kind of film. Not some deep and powerful film that moves you, like *The Bicycle Thief* or *Brief Encounter.* Not even a sentimental classic, like *Carousel* or *It's a Wonderful Life*. I mean some Lifetime channel made-for-TV menopause drama that you stumble upon in the middle of the night. Some embarrassingly manipulative estradiol-targeted story with predictable yet random tragedies, with kids and infidelity and self-pity. Some horribly tawdry thing, but it gets you. It just gets you, it makes it all just pour out of you. And after it is over, you feel as though you have really been through it. But what, really, have you been through? It is an exhausting and lonely moment, the moment the crappy movie is over and you are left with the crappy hollow feeling. That's what this feeling reminded me of. A small, meager experience that costs you way more than it ought to.

Not coincidentally, that crap feeling also reminds me of the feeling I would get after surfing the internet for three hours straight, tracing down information about, say, depression or ovarian cysts or halitosis, until I finally forgot what I wanted or what time it was. Until I finally turned off the computer and realized I had accomplished nothing but the slow suffocation of time.

It is the feeling that your life has just left the room.

There were four hyperpervious moments between the New Year's Day incident and my final crisis with Nik. I list them from least intense to most intense.

~~FRAGILE BORDER MOMENT #1~~
BREAKING EVENT #1

The rubescent drunk woman with the newborn baby who gets apprehended at a dive bar on New Year's Eve (insert description from my previous entry for January 1, 2004, but omit date).

BREAKING EVENT #2

I wasn't sure at first what I caught in the crawl at the bottom of the screen. As the news host interviewed an expert about an entirely different subject, the words creeping underneath them said, BREAKING . . . GARRET WAYNE, STAR OF *THE K.O.* AND LATER HOST OF *MAKE ME AN OFFER*, SHOT HIS WIFE AND SON BEFORE KILLING SELF . . .

That was it. The people above kept talking about some flooding in the Midwest. Then the crawl changed: SHIITE LEADER AYATOLLAH SISTANI REFUSED TO MEET WITH U.S. OFFICIALS TODAY . . . NASDAQ FINISHED UNDER 2000 IN HEAVY TRADING . . .

I clicked to another channel. There it was, home footage of Garret Wayne in his backyard. He is swimming in his pool with his sweet five-year-old son and his tall blond wife. They are smiling and waving. Garret is tan and glistening in the sun; his torso is etched and there is no sign of career dissipation in his abdominal muscles. I couldn't help but think it—this family looks so good, so happy, so beautiful.

And I started crying, which felt ridiculous, because I didn't know Garret Wayne, his blond wife, or his beautiful son. But it had been a long day, I was tired, and I couldn't stop. The people talking had no information, no explanation, but they kept on anyway. They talked about the pressures of stardom, or the pressures of losing stardom. But then they showed a picture of Garret Wayne as a teenage star. His hair was blow-dried and he looked very young. This was how I remembered him. I had a small, stupid crush on him when I was eleven. Before I decided I was cool and loved only David Bowie. Before I was cool, I was eleven and I loved Garret Wayne. I loved his girly looks and his slim, tapered waist. I loved his shy, almost secret smile. Before I loved the pale, druggy ennui of the rock boys, I loved the all-American Garret Wayne. So I cried.

They were showing Garret in the pool again. He waves, dives in, and surfaces with a toss of wet hair and a grin. He reaches for his son. His wife helps the boy jump into his father's arms. Then they all smile and wave again. I realized this must be the only footage they have of the whole family. I realized they will be showing this over and over again. They cut to some people talking, but they kept playing the home movie in a little box in the corner of the screen. Above the crawl, which continued on to floods, wars, and stock prices. Then a commercial came.

I clicked over to another channel. My hyperemotional reaction began to disgust me. I had, in middle age, become a person whose deepest emotional moments happened vicariously. Which reminded me again of my preteen years. How then I also lived through others, how I was dominated by fantasy. My emotional life nothing except what I longed for. And I remembered my feelings, sexual, sure, but more accurately described as presexual. I would imagine just holding hands with Garret Wayne, just being his girlfriend, just going to his house in Hollywood. The hand-holding was erotic and physical, but a lot of the fantasy was material: I imagined living in his big house and getting nice jewelry from him. Oh God. I was not particularly deep at eleven. I cried about what a deeply pathetic person I was. How can something so banal, so cliché, bother me so? Worn out from trying to resist it, I let myself sob: a fat, audible, nose-dripping sob.

I cried even more as I watched a stupid, hastily assembled montage of Garret on another channel. Here he is in *The K.O.*, the seventies TV series that made his name. He played the son of a renegade former law enforcement officer, a default private detective in a quasi-vigilante mode. He would hang around with his dad, played first by a squinty-eyed Scott Glenn and then later by an equally squinty Jan-Michael Vincent. They would drive along dusty highways in their Pontiac GTO convertible and escape the pursuit of a dark, unknown syndicate of government and organized crime operatives as they avenged average and grateful citizens across America, but usually somewhere out west with dusty roads. They would always move on at the end of the episode, because they had to, because they were being chased, but often leaving a perfectly good woman behind, often with a perfectly good daughter by her side, making meaningful eye contact with young Garret Wayne. It was a big show, but I really watched it only the first three years. In the fifth season, the nineteen-year-old Garret was on his own, his father killed by the syndicate and its unseen monolithic force of cowards. The show was canceled after the limping, played-out sixth season.

Of course I understood how we suffuse random external events with the spiritual weight of our own emotional lives as a way to feel things without ever really understanding them. We feel for the wrong things and for the wrong people, and so we are never released. But that didn't stop me; it just gave my overreactions a little niggle of self-loathing, a weary gnaw of guilt.

They were showing the clip of Garret in the backyard again. He was forty-nine years old, but he looked much younger. He looked much younger than I did, and I was—Jesus Christ—forty-seven years old. He'd had some amazing plastic surgery, the kind that didn't show, the kind that made you look like the best possible version of your age. How shameful, how awful, to hear about a tragedy and relate it to my vanity and insecurity about aging. I was so full of self-reproach and disgust, I lost track of what was on and found myself watching commercials. I grabbed the remote; I pressed.

They were showing Garret in his backyard. He must be in Beverly Hills. His wife's name was Elaine. She was thirty-four. They were separated. She reportedly had a problem with depression. He reportedly had a problem with prescription drugs. They were now talking about Gig Young, who shot himself and his wife in the seventies. But someone basically was saying this beats that because Gig Young didn't also shoot his five-year-old son. But someone else was saying, not really, because Gig Young had won an Oscar, and Garret Wayne was pretty much a washed-up has-been TV actor—they didn't actually say that, but they pretty much did.

He smiles at the camera, he smiles at his wife. She's glistening in the sun, her legs are long and taper perfectly to her knees. She is shiny and he is shiny and he dives in. She helps the laughing little boy jump off the edge into his father's waiting arms. His waiting arms, outstretched. I have memorized the rhythm of this family moment. It was cliché and predictable and clearly fake. It was unbearably, meaninglessly sad. I cried. How could I not cry?

I turned off the TV and, instead of going to bed, I went to my computer. I checked my email. I checked Ada's blog. It hadn't been updated since earlier in the week. I sent her an email just to say hi. Then I did it, I typed Garret's name into the search box. Thousands of hits came up. And I went in, clicking on one site after another, going back to the search list so I didn't miss anything. I didn't find much I didn't already know. He had a website, so I looked at that, but it wouldn't load because it had too many hits. I understood that I was only one of tens of thousands of people following these links, going to these websites, sitting exhausted in front of a computer. I ended up at a hastily assembled tribute site, watching clips of Garret from *The K.O.* Tons of comments, many posted that very hour. In fact, although the site was put up that day, it already had thousands of visitors. I was alone and yet right there among thousands of people. We were all together in our puerile, lurid nostalgia, yet we were sitting all alone. It was no comfort, really, it just made it worse. By the next week—at the latest—this would all be quiet and abandoned. A relic site.

I went to bed, exhausted and depressed.

For days, I would return to the Garret story. I checked the tribute site, but after a week it stopped getting new posts. The story dropped away, just an autopsy toxicology report of the various substances in the bodies' bloodstreams. I didn't care about that, how the contents of your blood became public information. I just thought about, and could not stop thinking about, what Garret Wayne's last day was like. Did he get up and think, This will be the last day of my life? Or did he fall into a sudden rage, a rage of such distortive, annihilating force that he couldn't stop himself? Was the gun sitting in a drawer, just in case? I stared at the headshot photo of his actress wife that had become ubiquitous now. Did she know what was coming? If not, how was that possible? I stared into the artfully lit eyes of this pretty, ordinary girl and tried to see if her future was written in her face.

We all long to escape our own subjectivity. That's what art can do, give us a glimpse of ourselves connected with every human, now and forever, our disconnected, lonely terms escaped for a moment. It offers the consolation of recognition, no small thing. But what the televised bombardment of violent events did to me was completely different. I didn't overcome my subjectivity; rather, my person got stretched to include the whole world, stretched to a breaking point. I became pervious, bruised and annihilated. That's what it feels like, this debilitating emotional engagement—annihilation, not affirmation.

I finally made myself fall into bed.

BREAKING EVENT #3

It happened as I was eating in front of the television news. I know this was asking for it, I know, but this is what people who live alone often do. I was tired and couldn't bother with the paper. I didn't even want the commitment of a movie. Mostly, then, I watched the news.

A breaking story was in progress. Everything was always in progress and yet still breaking. The cable news people were discussing a missing child. Since I had just tuned in, they worked hard to catch me up on what was now unfolding. This wasn't some suburban child stolen from a backyard in California. This was a thirteen-year-old Amish girl from a community in upstate New York. A box in the corner of the screen showed a live shot of a quiet dusty road with some patched farm hills in the background. When they moved to a full screen of the live shot for a reporter's update, I could barely make out a church steeple silhouetted against the distant mountains. The update was: no updates yet, but they never say that. They were interviewing random, non-Amish locals.

Nobody, it was clear, had a clue. Then they had an Amish expert on to talk. While she spoke, they showed stock footage of a buggy with a fluorescent orange safety triangle on it as the professor explained what Old Order Amish believed. What technologies they resisted. Why they refused to be interviewed on camera. They also brought on a missing-children expert. They spent minutes repeating, in different ways, the total lack of clues. But what trumped all of this information about the lack of information and showed clearly the reason we were all so deeply concerned was what they did actually have: a photo of her, the missing girl. A single gorgeous photograph apparently from a feature in a glossy magazine where the photographer had taken striking close-up portraits of rural Americans, particularly Amish and Mennonites. Amish usually don't let themselves be photographed (said the Amish expert—the headline read "Plain People" as he spoke). Amish believe photographs encourage vanity.

Yes, yes. I put a forkful of brown rice in my mouth. Clearly that was one of the many dangers in photographs; and yet here was this rather exceptional photo of this girl. It is an intimate shot, not awkward or posed at all. She is carrying a bucket and the weight of it has pulled her arms down and forward toward the camera. She wears a sheer white cotton bonnet. The ties are undone and hang like hair down the sides of her face. A few strands of blond hair escape the edge of the bonnet and soften her cheek. Her eyes are wide-set, pale and clear. But she has the tiniest hint of something hard to fix in her expression—a delicate wisp of mystery, as if her fragile lips might be about to smile. She didn't look childish or even very pretty. She just attended the moment—the camera's moment—in a way that looked intensely present. She seemed like a real person, not a "missing Amish girl," as the caption under the photo proclaimed.

I tried to not read the crawl underneath: ARNOLD PALMER BOWS OUT OF MASTERS . . . NBA HORNETS@HEAT 7:00 . . . ST. JOSEPH'S COLLAPSES AGAINST XAVIER . . . But I kept catching things, and then I would follow to catch up as the letters slipped off to the left: KE TYSON NOT TO RETURN TO THE RING: "TOO OLD, TOO TIRED" . . .

Live coverage of the Montgomery County sheriff's press conference was coming up. Only the commercials released me from the odd back-and-forth between the ticker crawling beneath and the incongruent images above it. It offered, I suppose, a way to never leave anything out. Maybe it was supposed to make you feel you could continue watching this show and you would miss nothing. You don't need to surf, we will surf for you. We could cover something deeply and endlessly, yet we would leave nothing else out. But instead it made you feel that you were always missing more and more. The endlessness of it, the abundance of it, the pace of it: it made me feel terribly anxious. Why is so much happening all the time? Why can't I stop it and read it? Why aren't you pretending only one thing matters at a time, why aren't you helping me make order of all of this? They began those crawls on 9/11 for emergency information. Like many emergency measures, it had become permanent. And it scattered my attention in uncomfortable ways.

The photograph fascinated me, but I wasn't that compelled to this story, not yet. The people kept talking about the Amish, and a box on the screen now showed the empty podium where the sheriff would soon appear. While we waited, they cut to a reporter interviewing another non-Amish resident of Montgomery County. Apparently, Amish are very nice . . . MOKTADA AL-SADR . . . BUSH $180 MILLION, KERRY $79 MILLION IN 1ST QTR FUND-RAISING REPORTS . . . they don't trust our modern conveniences but . . . OPRAH THANKS STAFF . . . help neighbors . . . WEEKLONG ALL-EXPENSE-PAID . . . plain people who put God and community first . . . GIBSON'S PASSION GETS BIG EASTER BO . . . Amish are wary of strangers . . . WORKERS FILE LAWSUIT AGAINST ELITE SPA . . . children like to play games just like non-Amish children, whom they call "English" . . . WHITE HOUSE RELEASES AUGUST 01 MEMO SAID TO WARN OF ATTACK "IN THE UNITED STATES" . . . G.E. BACKS 1ST QTR EARNINGS FORECAST AS GLOBAL ORDERS FOR APPLIANCES, SILICONE, AND SECURITY PRODUCTS REBOUND . . . *Good afternoon—*

At last the sheriff was now speaking LIVE. And no one knows anything or says anything new. Just seeing Amish people filmed from the back or from afar as they got discussed on the cable news made me uncomfortable enough, but the full breaking point didn't hit me until the next evening.

When I got home from work, the house felt very quiet. I turned on the news, and there they all were, seemingly unchanged from the night before. They continued because the story hadn't played out yet. No body, no crime, not yet. But they really continued because they had something new, and this was the breaking point: they secured an interview with the mother of the girl. I knew (from all the experts I heard yesterday) that Amish people don't go on TV. She was breaking *Ordnung* rules for humility and could be shunned or excommunicated. Inexplicably, while we waited for the exclusive interview, the little box in the corner showed a barn raising from the film *Witness*. Next the entire screen switched to a detailed map of the abduction site with the photo of the missing Amish girl in a box and an 800 number for tips on the ticker.

Then the mother appeared in a dark blue bonnet and dark blue dress and cape. She stood next to the reporter, and the sheriff stood behind her. The reporter asked why she was going on TV, and after a long pause, she answered. She wanted to help find her daughter Annie. She is thirteen and five feet two inches tall and weighs one hundred pounds. She was wearing a gray dress with a white apron. The woman spoke with an odd German torque, a hard-up inflection at the ends of the words. She was not beautiful. She was not the picture of Amish beatitude. She trembled. She looked down, she appeared frightened. Her voice shook, and then she couldn't speak any longer. She glanced up one last time and shook her head a tiny bit as she looked into the camera. Her eyes were the same as her daughter's, I could see that, but rubbed and red at the edges. I tried to imagine what she saw, or what she imagined the world saw. How did she conceive of the world through the camera and beyond her village? The journalist interviewing her almost reached for the woman as she backed away, and the moment was odd and raw. Her desperate capitulation to the harsh calculus of the English world that had swallowed her child would be endlessly repeated. Her resistance to humility in the face of God's will would play over and over. Then it was gone and it was back to the thousand volunteers scouring the bleached late-winter hillside. The suspicious neighbor. The humble ways of these quiet people. Amish girls are seldom alone . . . KERRY VETTING POSSIBLE VICE PRESIDENTIAL CANDIDATES.

This one would not be let go for a while. They had that photograph of the girl (now etched in my brain forever). And they had that video of the mother. Over and over, but then it would fade to the next thing. Not fade, it really was all and then nothing. Unless a body turned up, or a missing girl. By tomorrow evening, it would all be gone.

I didn't go to my computer. There would be time for that later on. I crept into the hottest tub of water I could stand. I lay down until the water covered me up to my neck. I leaned my head back against the porcelain. I cried until my eyes swelled and my face ached. I had been crying all along; as soon as the woman spoke, the tears started spilling down my face. My eyes were weary and swollen. The hot water felt good. I pressed a washcloth against my eyes.

Jay called. I didn't pick up the phone. I knew how ridiculous it sounded whenever I tried to explain to anyone—Ada, Nik, Jay—what made me so sad. No one is going to comfort you for what you saw on the news.

BREAKING EVENT #4

Wait, stop. There were several very significant others, but this recitation doesn't get it. It falsifies it somehow by rupturing it from the time between. It makes it cute. Or cynical.

Denise took off her glasses and pressed her palms to her eyes. No, things didn't happen in isolation. Ordering by chronology is better than ordering events by category. Things happened in a context, didn't they? Those breaking events happened to her, or affected her, because (maybe) of what surrounded them. It wasn't all events, it was some events. And maybe the why wasn't contained in the event itself but in her. How to get at that, then? Collage? Pastiche? A list? Rhetorical questions? Or tell a story?

She had to eat something. It was drafty. She pulled on one of Nik's black sweaters. All his clothes were black. He didn't have a lot, at least not in his bureau. He had a lot of canned food. Organic chili. He bought organic canned food? That lacked a certain amount of derring-do for a drinking-smoking-pill-popping rock and roller. She laughed, and that was how she felt: giddy, high, on the verge of tears or laughs. A crazy person.

She heated the food and then ate fast, standing up. She was in a rush. She longed to get back to the writing. She wanted only that: to keep going. She surrendered to her mania, her hypergraphic state, and she couldn't make herself stop until she had finished.

APRIL 2–14, 2004

Back to the calendar of linear events. The advantage of some agreed-upon measure to shape the past is hard to argue against. For instance, I remember what happened between April 1, April Fools' Day, and April 15, tax day. Now I regret what happened that day, but there was, I think, a very specific context to what transpired. I was getting my papers together for my tax returns. In exchange for allowing me some flexibility, my wealthy boss paid me as an independent contractor, meaning I was responsible for my own self-employment taxes and had to keep track of all possible expenses. I was sitting cross-legged on the floor with receipts, bank statements, utility bills, mortgage statements, insurance bills, and credit card statements arranged in little stacks all around me. I sorted and I felt the soul-sucking weariness of counting money long spent. The phone rang.

"Good, you're home. I'm a few minutes away, can I stop by?"

"Yeah, but I'm in the middle of sorting crap for my taxes."

Nik couldn't possibly be in the area by accident; I lived forty miles northeast of him, forty traffic-thick, developer-contrived nowhere sprawly miles. There was no reason to be there unless you lived there, unless you decided you wanted to go for a drive on a congested freeway to shop at Best Buy or Bed Bath &

Beyond instead of going to your nearby neighborhood shopping mall and shopping at Best Buy or Bed Bath & Beyond.

Nik walked with a slight limp across my paper-strewn living room. He opened the sliding glass door to the patio and lit a cigarette. He stared at the piles of papers on the floor. He took off his sunglasses and rubbed his eyes and his chin. I could see he hadn't shaved in a while: his beard was not ever all that heavy, and he had to skip shaving for a couple of days for anything to really show.

I got up from my stack of receipts and went into the kitchen. The whole house was built on a one-level horizontal line facing southwest. The kitchen opened to the dining room, which was open to the living room in a sort of L shape. It was an old-fashioned California suburban setup, built for fair-weather, optimistic middle-class comfort. The modest square footage didn't feel too small because the two bedrooms off the hall and the main living space all faced the patio and were accessible to it through sliding glass doors. The orientation to the sliding glass doors and the outside beyond the doors also made it feel as if there were no distinct spaces, so I could make coffee in the kitchen and still talk to Nik by the patio door. He reached in his coat and pulled out a thick manila envelope.

I knew what was coming, I had seen it before. I wasn't in the mood for making it easy.

"How's your foot?" I said.

"Much better, actually. Thank you."

"Did you see Dr. Fillmore?"

"Yeah. You were right, it is a kind of arthritis. He gave me some medication."

I nodded as I poured myself a cup of coffee before the maker had stopped brewing. The coffee dripped from the filter onto the exposed burner, sizzled, and instantly smelled burnt. This would be my third cup of afternoon coffee.

"Good," I said. I had given Nik the $150 for the doctor. I knew he also had a $975 bill from the emergency room. He would ignore that.

"How's work?" he said. I just stared at him.

"How is your work?" I said.

"Great—see for yourself," he said, holding out the manila envelope to me.

"I mean your job, have you—"

"I missed almost two weeks. I still can't work too much. I can't stand for long."

I sighed.

"But you know, Dave is very cool about it, he lets me sit most of the shift."

I poured milk in my coffee and stirred it. I didn't look at him.

"I'm broke myself right now," I said, frowning and stirring. "I don't really have it. I mean, I really don't."

"Of course," he said, "I know that. I'm not asking you."

He put out his cigarette. He smiled and opened the envelope he had been holding out to me and pulled out a CD case. "Guess what? What you have been waiting for, hoping for—a new Fakes bootleg. Very rare. I've had a lot of time to work, so I compiled it this week. The unreleased 2004 sessions, made exclusively for you." He handed it to me.

"How much do you need?" I said, ignoring the CD.

He shrugged and waved his hand. "A thousand," he said.

"The whole rent, Nik? You don't have any of it?"

"That's not the *whole* rent. My rent is twelve hundred." He reached in his jacket pocket for another cigarette. "You don't need to worry about it. I have things in motion," he said.

"I thought you worked some shifts," I said.

He exhaled. "I had to buy food and gas, too." And cigarettes and scotch, I thought. At least I didn't say that to him. I marched over to my desk. I pulled open a drawer. I riffled through the papers until I found a credit card offer that included some low-interest-rate checks attached to a piece of paper upon which many caveats, warnings, catches, and asterisks (which I supposed meant risks of a sidereal nature) were printed in the classic credit card tiny faint print. The first time you actually read the words printed on these things was to feel the last connection to your childhood die. I filled one out for a thousand dollars. I handed it to him. He folded the check and put it in his billfold.

"I'm grateful, but you don't need to do it."

"Nik, this is truly it. You gotta figure something out. I'm in over my head here. I'll fucking never pay off what I owe." This was a true statement.

He looked down, nodding.

"You have to do something, file for disability or *something*."

"I'm not even on the books for more than minimum wage, so disability wouldn't really help much."

"Well, we have to figure out something soon."

After he left, I put on Nik's fake illicit record. He had made a gorgeous little cardboard digipak for the CD. It was deliberately sort of rough, so it would look like a bootleg. He had several fake "unauthorized" labels; this was a Mountebank

Industries release, which meant it was acoustic demos, not a live concert bootleg, which would be, if it were the Fakes and not the Demonics (and never Nik Worth solo because he never played live), on the Cold Slice label. Nik said he had to tolerate these little sub-rosa products—after all, the fans demanded more than the bands could officially release.

The record is some wounded lyrical pop called *Breakfast at Kingdom Come.* It is just him with the piano or the guitar. No overdubs. His voice, totally naked and wrapped around a simple melody, sounds both familiar and strange. His uncanny lyrics always step up to surreal but never fall in. Just odd enough to mean something unusual. That's Nik— the songs sound off and unexpected, yet after a second listen, you are hooked and craving their delicate circles and little returns and secret crevices.

I left all my papers on the floor and went to bed. I couldn't sleep; drinking so much coffee had been a terrible idea. I lay there, closed my eyes, and tried to force my way into something approaching a rest state. My ill-considered sleep strategy was to mentally add up what I had given Nik over the years. Mostly the last ten years. The extravagant gifts, like the Canon color copier. (I had just received a home equity line of credit that I used to pay off my car and my credit card debts. I used the extra money to buy Ada a professional digital camera and Nik a top-of-the-line personal color copier. Of course both of those objects are more or less obsolete today. The massive credit card debt reaccrued.) I gave him money for rent on countless occasions. I gave him money for medical expenses. I gave him money for car repairs (uh, Nik, your tires look a little dangerous). He used to pay it back, but eventually we didn't bother to keep track. After all, my boss did pay me well, fairly good-sized lump checks that were so easy to spend. I used to help out my mother, too. At least now I didn't have to pay for things for her. Her low Social Security income and her age and her total lack of assets had made things much easier. I did have to spend hours calling agencies and filing paperwork for her, but I even managed to get her a home aide to shop for her and visit once a day through the state in-home services and Medi-Cal. And Ada's father paid for many of Ada's expenses. So why shouldn't I help Nik? Why should I offer him money he doesn't even ask for and then berate him? Why was I such a horrible and selfish person? How could I spend money on champagne for Ada when my brother needed money just for his life? What is wrong with me—did I always have to be so self-indulgent, so extravagant? But it wasn't really just extravagances, I had a high mortgage (and still lived at least an hour from everything). Some of that debt was spent on my insurance, my gas, my basic cost of living. I also had to pay, for instance, income taxes, property taxes—I didn't plan well and things always came up. I lived beyond my means, it was true, but that was not hard to do. If Nik needed money, what difference did it make if I spent another thousand or not? This kind of thinking explained how I had accumulated a tremendous amount of debt over the last eight years. My monthly payments were fast approaching an unsustainable level. Somehow the whole big monster just kept rolling forward. I wouldn't be able to pay it off unless I sold my house and moved to Alabama or Bakersfield or some other place where I could afford to buy a house with the pittance I would have left after I paid my debts. Which I couldn't do. Or I could sell my house and pay off my debt and then rent a place. But I was reaching the point where I had depleted my equity so completely that it was possible I might not break even when I sold my house.

I needed to get some sleep. Downward I plunged—just watch me, I won't stop.

I could file for bankruptcy. The ruptured bank option. Chapter 7, I should do it. But I wasn't behind yet, I managed it all somehow. I tried to comfort myself with options, tried to put these things into perspective. I redirected my thoughts, I focused on breathing in and out. To find my way to some rest. I gave up and took a blue oval tablet from a bottle containing a quick-acting nonbenzodiazepine hypnotic, a nonaddictive sleep aid. What we used to call sleeping pills but can't anymore because it sounds too tragic.

APRIL 20

Jay and I watched an early Peter Sellers movie. He had stopped with the James Mason movies just when I was trying to find a way to tell him how sick I was getting of watching the James Mason movies. Evidently James Mason made hundreds of movies, and they were not all *Lolita.* The idea of seeing each one of them might have worked as a stupid conceit in a novel, or as a bit of film-school-teacher shtick, but in realty, in praxis, such obsessions grow increasingly tedious. The experience does not increase in meaning by its devotion to thematic repetition, or mere accumulation. The stubborn concentration does not make your appreciation of James Mason deeper. Instead it increases one's intolerance and irritation. You grow to hate all James Mason movies, even the good ones.

Jay must have sensed my growing ambivalence, and today he switched to Peter Sellers without making any mention of or reference to the change. We watched *The Ladykillers,* which Jay found uproariously funny. We ate sushi as we watched. We drank Sapporo beer and the combination made our mouths taste funny. Later, we avoided kissing.

He still brought me Thomas Kinkade Painter of Light™ gifts. This obsession wasn't negotiable. They stacked up in my garage.

Also April 20

When Jay got up to use the bathroom, I checked my email. I knew from Ada's blog posts that she was moving forward with her documentary about Nik. I had been enthused and then began ignoring and nearly discouraging it for some reason.

hey ma,
guess what? i'm thinking I would come out and film in the next month. I know that is sooner than i said, but I have some investors to get me started—i will explain when i see you. dad will get me a ticket with his miles. Of course i would stay with you if i could, but you are so far away from everything. i will stay at Mike's house by Runyon Canyon—you know i want to film some of the movie there. I haven't talked to nik about the details of this yet. Did you get a chance to mention it to him and see what he thinks? do you mind? I would need to interview you, too, is that okay?
I'm totally excited!
xoxoxoxo
a.

I clicked on MARK AS UNREAD and watched it become bold new mail again. I would answer it in the morning. I would have to talk to Nik. Nik didn't use email. He had my old computer and printer, but he didn't subscribe to the internet. He was stubborn this way. Last Christmas, Ada set up a MySpace page for Nik. One of Nik's signature Fakes songs played as soon as the page opened, "Sugar Caves." The details of the page were a continuation of the Chronicles fiction, or at least

Ada's approximation of it. Nik seemed touched, but he quickly pointed out the inaccuracies. (He was a stickler for precision in his fictions. No continuity issues, no sloppiness. He would later hand her a typed list of errata to add as a sidebar to the page.)

"You could, you know, extend your whole project onto the internet. You know, it would be perfect for that, it would make it totally multidimensional, update it. You could even put up MP3s of all the music, reach a new audience. I could help you, you know."

Nik stared at her laptop. He read aloud, "'Thirty-plus solo records, with the additional recordings of the two main bands plus the side bands.'" He chuckled.

"I think it looks great," I said. But actually it was weird seeing Nik in the real world like this—the real world of the internet. I felt anxious about it, too exposed somehow.

Ada smiled and clicked on the next song, the Demonics' "Somersault."

"You would have to do a separate Demonics page, a Fakes page, a Nik Worth page, even pages for some of the side projects like the Pearl Poets and Lozenge. And then link them all together," Nik said. Lozenge was Nik's short-lived one-man electro-boogie band.

"Exactly!" Ada said. "I could do that if you want."

Nik smiled at her. "Naw, not for me."

"Why?"

"Don't look so sad. It is just that I'm a paper-and-paste guy."

"A glitter-and-glue guy," I said.

"Yeah, that too."

I wasn't sure if Nik would want to have a documentary made

about him. But who knows, maybe he would jump at it. He had made lots of films and videos over the years. (First with our mother's Super 8 camera. Then a Betamovie camcorder I bought him for Christmas 1985. More recently a Sony MiniDV for his birthday.) He made music videos and a couple of clips where he interviewed himself. Ada could use all of that if she wanted. I didn't even know if she knew all the stuff that Nik had made over the years. I didn't even know it all.

Ada emailed me to tell me Nik had agreed to be interviewed. He agreed to open his archives to her. Whatever she wanted.

APRIL 24

It was eighty-one degrees and the midday sun seared me through the thin skin of my clothing. Despite my dark glasses, the blinding shine made phantom sunspots appear whenever I blinked. I helped her into the passenger seat and the oppressively stale and baked air of my car.

"Give it a minute." The car was on, the AC was on high, but it still only felt like the air pushed up to you and sat there, hot and thick. I knew that somewhere there were new cars that could do this air transition much better. But my mother didn't seem to notice. She sat and looked straight ahead. I drove out of the driveway of her apartment complex and toward the highway. We were on our way to Ralphs supermarket. Leslie, the home aide assigned to my mother, went shopping for her. But sometimes I went, and I took her with me. It was something to do, an activity. Usually we went to Wal-Mart, other times we went to Ralphs.

I pushed the cart. I had a small list. It felt nice and cool as we went down the aisle, and we were in no rush. She picked out cookies. And then some Pop-Tarts.

"Ma, you know you can't have too many sweets. You know, diabetes." She looked at me and sighed. She put the Pop-Tarts back, shoving them on the wrong shelf.

When I was a kid, I used to do exactly the same thing when I went shopping with my mother. I would try to slip sweets into our basket. We had so much food in our cart that sometimes it would work, and she wouldn't notice even at the checkout. She wouldn't notice until she unpacked it at home. I liked going with her to the supermarket, I used to ride underneath the basket of the shopping cart, sitting with legs straight out in front of me on the little shelf just above the wheels. She would push it for maybe an aisle, and then the wheels would catch and the cart would resist her push. She would tell me to get off and walk, it was too heavy. I would wander off and lose track of her. I didn't keep her in sight, because I had a system for finding her. I would walk along the end aisle and look up each lane until I found her. Once in a while I would get all the way to the end of the store and not see her. I would become slightly frantic, move quickly from aisle to aisle, and then get very frantic when I still couldn't find her. I would run to a checkout girl and get my mother paged.

I was reminded of this childhood panic when I spent too long staring at a box of cereal. I was reading labels, trying to see what she could eat within her diabetes guidelines. I looked up and she was gone. I left the cart and went to the end of the aisle. I looked in each direction—I looked for her, in her powder-blue tracksuit and her short gray hair. I didn't see her. I moved along, looking up each lane. Still I didn't see her. I felt myself panicking. I knew that one of the symptoms of dementia is "wandering." She could wander out into the street and disappear. It happened to old people all the time. They injure themselves, they get lost, they get hit by cars. I started to tear up as I hurried past all the lanes again. She wasn't that bad yet, she wasn't totally disoriented yet.

I saw her.

She was at the front of the store, on the other side of the checkout lines. She was standing with a police officer. I ran over, waving my arms at them. I saw that she had handcuffs on. My mother was in handcuffs.

"What is going on?" I said, still tearful, putting my arm around my mother. She looked at me, totally confused.

"Are you her daughter?" said the police officer, who I now saw was simply a security guard.

"Yes, I am. What is going on?"

"Your mother was shoplifting. When a clerk tried to stop her, she resisted him and shouted ethnic slurs," he said.

"My mother doesn't use ethnic slurs. And she doesn't shoplift. She probably just forgot to pay. She's old, you know?"

The guard undid the handcuffs. He claimed he just wanted to scare her a little. By handcuffing her in front of the entire store? She had put containers of yogurt in her pockets. And two candy bars up her sleeves. My mother had read the manager's identification pin and called him a dumb wop. She had no explanation for any of this behavior. They didn't press charges. I was told I could no longer bring my mother to the store. On the ride home, she muttered.

"What were you thinking?" I said, mostly rhetorically. She waved her hand at me and scowled.

"I've done it many times at that store," she said. "He always tries to bust me." I looked at her. Lately she had been experiencing déjà vu a lot. But, as I had discovered when I looked it up on SymptomSolve.com, what she actually was experiencing was called déjà vécu. Things are falsely familiar. You read the new experience of the moment as if it were a memory you were reliving. And you have no awareness of the falseness of the feeling. Fake memory. When I entered the term in the search engine, it was indexed to several kinds of dementia, epilepsy, and other prefrontal cortex diseases. But this behavior wasn't merely the déjà vécu. "What do you mean, he 'busts' you?"

"He shouldn't always try and shame me."

"No, he really shouldn't, I'm sorry about that."

"It doesn't work, because I don't care what people think. Certainly not some mick cop," she said.

I didn't know what to say. My whole life, I never heard my mother utter a single ethnic or racial epithet or even a stereotype. Mick? Wop? Where were these words coming from? You would think my mother spent her childhood as a Bowery Boy and not as the daughter of a Reseda shopgirl.

"They have been after me for a while. I know. You don't know what they have been up to. You don't know because you don't pay attention."

Where in her brain was this coming from? The doctor wasn't sure of the nature of her dementia, or how fast it would progress. He just called it likely Alzheimer's. He couldn't tell me what I could expect. Anything was typical. Anything was possible. At first I didn't think it really mattered—they were all equally untreatable. What difference did it make if it was this or that part of the frontal lobe? But I wasn't quite prepared for this latest sign of deterioration. It wasn't just forgetting the past or repeating the same thing over and over. It was actually remixing and changing the wiring. It was creating new things, it was changing her in real ways. She wasn't just losing her social inhibitions, nothing as benign as that. She was starting to get paranoid, and it made her someone else, someone a little mean. It just didn't seem fair.

That evening I spent hours on the internet reading about frontal temporal dementia. This led to cortical and subcortical dementias. And vascular dementias and the silent stroke events that can cause them, which also led me to TIDs, transient ischemic attacks or ministrokes. Then I read about cerebral infarctions. *Infarct* sounded like the perfect name for what I had just witnessed. And finding the perfect name seemed to mean I had accomplished something. But then I grew worried—had we missed a stroke event? Should I have taken her to the hospital? After twenty-four hours the neurological effects were irreversible. But then I read on and realized her symptoms didn't really match a stroke or TID or cerebral infarct after all, despite the apt-sounding name. I ended up back where I started, at the symptoms for frontal temporal dementia. I was going in circles. Pages were highlighted on the search list with little numbers indicating what time I had looked at that page. 1:35. 1:58. Did my ending back where I started mean something? I clicked and printed, and none of it made me feel better or worse. It just made me feel tired.

In the coming weeks, my mother would seem almost her old self. Fatigue made her symptoms worse. But there was no doubt that things progressed in one direction. Her doctor suggested we move her to nearby (to me) assisted living (that also accepted

Medi-Cal). I would have to fill out the paperwork and get her on the waiting list.

Sometimes I printed things out to read later and then never got around to reading them. Other times I would read what I had printed the night before, or a week before. This time I read as I drank my morning coffee and ate my breakfast whole-grain toast. Frontal temporal dementia, FTD, the one she had the symptoms for, was naturally the dementia most strongly linked to hereditary causes. One form of it—yet another subcategory to explore—causes aphasia. *Aphasia*, the gentle-sounding word has a Greek etymology that means moving away from speech toward muteness. A seemingly blissful silence, almost. But aphasia actually means the forgetting of language, the loss of using and understanding language altogether, either specific words or syntax or both—and can present in the patient as early as her forties.*

*erratam note

I have forgotten to include something, and this feels like a relevant place to correct the record. I am taking her meds. I TAKE MY MOTHER'S PILLS. No, I'm not taking them from her; I am also taking them. She has a giant six-month supply of galantamine, her quasi-effective anti-Alzheimer's pills, endlessly refillable. So what is the harm? Why not take a prophylactic dose myself? I filled her plastic container that had a little compartment for each day of the week. She had a morning set and an evening set. One day, not so long ago, when I was filling it, it occurred to me: Why not take it myself? It can't hurt. I doled out, every week, handfuls of supplements and filled the compartments to the brim. In addition to her doctor's prescribed galantamine, I added piracetam, choline, alpha-lipoic acid, vinpocetine. I scoured the World Wide Web for possibilities. I bought them in bulk and they were still significant hits on my credit card. I hated the names that appeared on my statements: memextend, nusmart, braintonics, mindroids, movita. As if smooshing words together and eliminating any tongue-tripping syllables somehow hit just the right promissory key.

She often forgot to take them. Noncompliant. Well, of course she was noncompliant. How could she remember to take her memory pills? But I was totally compliant. I took the same memory-enhancing regimen I had cobbled together for her. I felt foolish doing it; what exactly was I so desperate to retain? Didn't I see she could be released, stoic, alive only to the moment? I no longer had peaceful moments in my days, I just had these desperate backward grasps.

Writing it all down, and for what, exactly?

APRIL 25

lowercase a:
daily musings of an unemployed but brilliant filmmaker
Okay, I am heading out to LA to start filming my documentary, Garageland. Garageland *is about a life spent making music and art outside of the mainstream. Way outside. It is a celebration of a devoted unrepentant eccentric. It is about living out a secret fantasy life of your own making. Do you need an audience to create work, or does not having an audience liberate you and make you a truer artist? And ultimately,* Garageland *will question what makes a person produce in the face of resounding obscurity. We have enough money for our initial budget. We will shoot enough to put together twenty minutes and then use that to get more investors and, hopefully, a distributor. If you would like to be an investor (yes, you can produce films), join our DIY efforts. You can invest/contribute through your Paypal account here.*
a

He would be interviewed and he would open his archives to her. He was willing, it seemed, or at least indifferent enough, to go along with it. Nik hardly ever said no, he just slid out of things. Anyway, the chances were slim that she would raise enough money to make a full-length movie, so what could be the harm in letting her film him? I didn't realize the uncertain alchemical potential of filmic attention. Or of any attention. But maybe part of me did.

Ada had gone to her father, Chris. He would at least give her some starting funds. I knew he would help her—that's just who Chris is. Chris worked as an information systems manager and lived in a split-level ranch in Huntington Beach with his wife and two small children. Chris lived as normal a life as one could imagine. Who knows, of course, but he appeared content, and how could I want anything less for him? We were so long past as to almost never have been, save for Ada and her brilliant reordering of the best of our genetic attributes. And a person was not a small thing, as far as things between people go. So here we were, Chris and I, never seeing each other but deeply in each other's life.

When I first met him, Chris played bass in this eyeliner band called Ether. (Later they moved from New Romantic/new wave to a more death/Goth style and changed their name to the Select and then, after Chris left, to Crown of Thorns. After that they moved beyond death/Goth to life/bright wave and then to Romanesque edge metal and changed the name to Leviathan until they finally broke up or faded out or quietly kept going in someone's garage.)

They were not good.

He played bass and he sang in an uncomfortable nasal tenor. His singing didn't match him—he should have been short and slight with missing teeth and a dirty mohair sweater. He was too pretty for his voice, for the band, and way too pretty for the scene. 1980 was a tiny window of a moment when pretty boys were suspect. Chris was more suited to be an actor than a singer. For one thing, he smiled all the time, his huge brown eyes clearly discernible despite the hunk of brown hair that he used to comb over half his face. He wore tons of kohl on his eyes, and he wore earrings and even feathers in an unlucky pirate/Indian amalgam.

Despite all his miscalculations, he was beautiful.

I was one of those girls who loved boys who looked like girls. As far as I was concerned, the gayer a guy looked, the better. A guy couldn't be too gay-looking for me at that point. Gay, gay, gay. It was my version of anti-sex, I suppose, to be in love with gay boys. But I really did love them and want them. I had spent from sixteen to nineteen having a lot of sex. Most of it wasn't great. I don't even remember all the men I had sex with in those days. It used to make me cringe, but now I sort of admire my shameless promiscuous period. I would go out and get wasted and then wait until someone made a move on me. I usually had a few to choose from, but I was pretty ecumenical in my selections. I would go to their house or, I'm afraid, their car. And if I liked the sex, I would stick around and see the guy again. Sometimes, like with this one seemingly sweet guy, Brad, the feelings between us would disappear after sex. He asked me home after we shouted into each other's ears for an hour over bourbon and room-shaking bass. We both agreed the band was great, or awful, or boring. We made out in the parking lot behind the club—I think it was the Starlight, or Van's, or the Velvet Pony. He drove us to his studio apartment in Silver Lake. He looked younger in the light of his kitchen. We smoked a joint. We had tender stranger sex, his broad hand guiding my lower back. A sigh in my ear. And I remember feeling that we worked well together, we lacked the common awkwardness and the itchy discomforts of new bodies. Afterward—right afterward—he unpeeled himself, sat up, and lit a cigarette. He wouldn't speak or look at me until I left. I had to call Nik for a ride.

Other times, like with this other guy whose name I won't recall, we started out almost nasty in bed—he whispered all the porn things he could think of into my ear as he held me down. Of course I discovered this was the kind of guy who ends up falling hard: calling all the time, then following me, writing notes and then letters, until I actually had to hide from him.

My sex life often felt complicated and unpleasant. Then, after one too many postcoital waves of despair, I had a change of inclination. I became what some people call a fag hag.

I used to think I liked gay men because I could remain safely undesired with them. I wanted to avoid sex. That was an aspect of it. But now I realize it was also because I loved men too much. I loved being around them before they played with their band and after, I loved joking with them, and I loved getting high with them. I loved how they loved music and pool and how they harbored secret ambitions. I loved the size of their hands and, truly, I loved how they all wanted sex all the time. Somehow (perhaps mistakenly) I never perceived this as predatory; I thought their constant desire made them needful and secretly vulnerable. I felt almost sorry for them. What I learned after a couple of years as a hard-core free girl is that if I really liked a guy, I shouldn't have sex with him. One of us (unclear who beforehand) would want more than the other one did. It is weird, and lovely, how sex changes everything, how there is no predicting what will happen until you're there on the other side with your swollen lips and unrolling your underwear from the bunched top sheet. Except you could predict that you wouldn't be friends afterward. It was extremely unlikely that it would feel the same to both of you. Therefore, if I really liked a guy, sleeping with him would ensure he would not be in my life very long.

So why didn't I just stay friends with straight guys and not sleep with them? Because even if you didn't sleep with them, sex came up and interfered. For example, I didn't want to sleep with my friend James: he was my good buddy; he made me laugh; our sensibilities matched perfectly; and we could and would stay up all night talking. We even watched movies together over the phone, adding constant commentary as we watched. Eventually, the moment came, as it always did. He'd had a few drinks. He clutched my hand. I knew what was coming. I could feel how he wouldn't forgive me. He thought I didn't sleep with him because I was shallow and wanted only aloof, unattainable men. I could feel, and see in his face, as his desire quickly slid into resentment. Now I was using him, getting all the companionship without giving up any of the goods. Then I was a tease, and finally, of course, a bitch.

But with gay men it was all different. They were not trying to get on you or even thinking about getting on you. You were not trying to get on them. You were not waiting to convert them. Not at all. Gay men you could love without hesitation, without jeopardizing your friendship, without art or guile. I still kind of feel this way. True, I never got actual sex from them, but I got to dance, I got to lean against them, I got to hold hands, I even got to sit in a lap or two. We could ironically ape straight couples. I could still admire the large hands, or the curve of a shoulder, or the way a male back looked under a T-shirt. Contrary to the fag-hag cliché, we did not merely discuss male movie stars in salacious terms. We might have shared an appreciation for the male form, but that was only one small part of it. It really was about pure male companionship, something I couldn't get from straight men or women of any tendency. Who knows what they got out of it (perhaps easy friendship and a little comfort), but gay men became my default favorites in those days. Aside from my brother, they were the only men whose desire I didn't have to worry about.

I knew right away Chris was gay. The way he coquettishly leaned backward against the bar behind him, pushing up the unbuttoned cuffs of his white rayon shirt. It was actually more of a blouse than a shirt. He asked me for a cigarette. I watched him as he lit his cigarette and took a drag. I could see a triangle of taut flesh where his half-tucked-in blouse fell open at the hem; it created an inviting slide of rayon each time he moved. Although he was skinny, he was more muscular than the average rock guy—he probably did push-ups every day (GAY). He teetered on the heel of a boot and slouched sleepily to one side. He glanced at me as I stared at him, and he smiled broadly, a real grin. In contrast to him, I wore a long-sleeved T-shirt and jeans and boots with a vintage crepe dress pulled over the whole ensemble. Between my makeup and clothes, I didn't show an inch of flesh or form. I liked it, me covered and desexed, him revealed flesh and smiles.

He was near enough to me that I could smell sandalwood incense and, faintly under that, soap. Just another gorgeous gay boy. He was even a little bit tan, which was completely recherché for straight rock boys in those days. But mostly I located his gayness in the artifice of his presentation, his shameless and flamboyant poseur-tude.

I kept thinking how gay he was while he yanked my jeans and panties off as I lay laughing on his bed. My hand was in his hair as his mouth pressed and licked, both gentle and insistent, and I thought, *This is the gay way to fuck a girl, right?* Even though that was clearly unlikely. I thought of him as gay as we met up night after night, invariably making out in a corner, or a car, or a parking lot, his hands searching for a way through my fortress of clothes. He gave me a coquettish smile as he took my hand and pulled me toward his car. Chris had (and has) no edge; he was happy and easy. And he wasn't, I finally understood, gay.

Nik thought Chris was a brainless pretty boy, but that wasn't right. He was very smart, he just wasn't dark. He came from a middle-class family in the Valley, and he had gone to private school. Yet he thought of himself as poor. I would have found that obnoxious in most people, but it seemed merely innocent in Chris. He was so comfortably not poor that he was able to take his background for granted and imagine us all in the same boat. He just didn't know what it meant to have no one to borrow from if you really needed money. He didn't know what it meant to have nothing under you or ahead of you, and he didn't understand what a difference that made. He was, assuredly, always broke, but it was a phase. He had a nice car (a 1980 Honda Accord) and his folks paid the insurance. "That's all," he said. He had gone to college and had no debt. He had insurance and a small untouchable fund for a future down payment on a house. That's all!

Chris didn't want Ada at first. Our infatuation was already on the wane—we were not broken up but on the way there. I had already had an abortion in high school. I was twenty-two, I was sure I would get another one. But somehow I found I just didn't want to. This pregnancy felt different. I knew (in the way women often claim to just know things and freak men out) that this was the baby I had to have. I knew. Somehow I believed that this would be my one chance to have a kid and I wouldn't get another. I had this certainty; maybe it was from hormones or perhaps wishful thinking as a way out of my wheel-spinning life. We didn't get married or even stay together, but Chris accepted my decision. He made arrangements. He gave me money every month until Ada was eighteen. He saw her regularly and he fell in love with her. He enjoyed, I think, being a dad but not having to do it full-time. Now-and-then dad. Naturally, Ada worshipped him. I didn't mind. She may have adored him more than anyone in the world, but I was like the air and the sun and the sea. I was the world.

APRIL 27

"I'm an ABAWD. An *aba-wod,*" Nik said.

"What's that?"

"Able-Bodied Adult Without Dependents. They don't like to give ABAWDs any help. They fingerprinted me and issued me an Electronic Benefit Transfer card."

Nik had finally signed up for food stamps. He got $108 a month, which wouldn't come close to making up for the shifts he could no longer work. He handed me the shiny food stamp credit card. It had a picture of pristine Pacific coastline on it. He took it back, slipped it in his wallet.

"At least you got something."

"Yes indeed."

I remember the moment when I first understood Nik and I had made real mistakes. Nik was in his early thirties or had just turned thirty. These were the years when my life was organized by Ada, my blundering and earnest care of Ada. I remember noticing, with real sadness, that we had strayed from an acceptable course, that our lives were going in the wrong direction. I actually thought those words, *how far we have strayed,* but I don't know if that was accurate. That would imply we were on the right course at some point.

We were having a pool party. The Maltman Avenue apartment complex where I was living at the time had a bright blue kidney-shaped swimming pool. In every respect, my Maltman apartment was horrible—the walls were thin drywall, the doors were hollow. At night I could hear arguing and fucking from all directions. This is what people don't realize unless they have lived it: the low-level indignities of a lousy, cheap apartment cloud your every moment. When I stood in the kitchen, I couldn't fully open the refrigerator door without hitting the edge of the stove. The plastic shower surround had permanent hard-water stains and moved when I leaned on it. Then there was the neutral-colored carpet and its odd petroleum smell. The sliding "natural wood" laminate shutter-styled closet doors that came off their rails each time I tried to open them. The popcorn ceiling I got to stare up at each night, and the odd layout contrived not for utility but only to fit the most in the least. It wasn't at all the same as living in an older run-down apartment. This apartment was old-new, and being brand-new was the only thing it ever had going for it. When Ada and I moved into our one-bedroom, it felt—the low ceilings, the dark hallways, the flimsy construction—old and used, maybe only five years old but old already. I accepted it because I believed it was temporary. Everyone did. No one wanted to imagine an entire life lived in that kind of space.

But the Maltman Avenue apartment complex did have one significant redeeming feature: the community pool in the center courtyard. It was perfectly fine, clean and full of chlorine. And no one really used it. Ada and I would have the pool to ourselves on hot afternoons, of which there were many. I taught her to swim, and it made up for a lot.

We were having a pool party. I was dating this guy Bill at the time. He was a lot older than I was. He made good money as a lighting technician, he was a member of IATSE Local 33. He was not my usual type, but he asked me out and we ended up together for almost two years. He liked how I looked—I think that was mostly it—and he seemed charmed by our many differences, at least at first. I thought I was being practical. But he liked to tell me what to do, and when he drank too much, he would say perceptive things like "You sure got it all figured out, don't you?" His low-grade sarcasm didn't hurt me, it just made me feel dull and tired. Bill did help Ada and me. He helped me with rent sometimes. He helped me with my car. I needed help.

This particular party had gone on too long. Everyone had been drinking all day in the sun. Ada—she was eight, maybe?—lay by the pool, eating potato chips and reading. I was high but not out of control. The day carried itself and kept going. I had finally persuaded Bill to cook the hamburgers and hot dogs on the grill. The ten or so people had eaten. The day was starting to fade into night, and people hung in there, talking, listening to music, drinking, disappearing and returning the way people do at a party. Ada, I remember, also had a little girlfriend there. Earlier they splashed in the pool, and now they lounged facedown on fluorescent pink beach towels, reading magazines and talking to each other. Foggily, or through a fog of party murmur, I heard a rise in the pitch of Bill's voice. I looked up at the stairs leading to our apartment, and there stood Bill and Nik. The volume of their argument escalated. They were nearly shouting. We all turned to look at them as the noise continued and rose above the music and conversation. We all stopped talking and watched them. A drunken, stupid argument. It was still daytime. The sun had not yet sunk out of view. I watched, Ada watched, we all watched as the men stopped pointing and shouting and stood back from each other. There was this evaporative moment, the moment when you could feel the violence in the air. Everyone was there with them, on the cusp. To watch it as it was happening made time seem to slow and also to collapse as I felt something rise in my chest and wave through my body. The intense autonomic discharge of frantic energy. It made me intake my breath sharply as though I were about to be hit.

"Go ahead," Nik said. He held open his hands, palms out. He had a queasy smile. He had the liberated, reckless glee of someone who knows what's coming. "Go ahead, you motherfucker."

Bill slammed his fist into Nik's face. A loud smack of skin with a cracking sound underneath. A sharp out breath, a yelp of pain. The fight was over. Bill stormed down the stairs. I shrieked at him. He left. Nik had a towel on his face, blood everywhere. And I knew, of course, that Ada and her friend had watched the whole thing. I could hear Ada crying. I held her and watched Lisa, Nik's girlfriend at the time, clean him up. Then I had this thought. This ugliness means something, this pointless ugliness in front of my child. Were we shameless, was that it? That must not have been it, because I felt a hot, deep shame. There were tears from shame. It wasn't that we were shameless, it was that we were careless. In that moment we had closed the distance between carefree and careless. Somehow, as we grew older, we lost our liberated, irresistible claim on being carefree. I felt it then, even if Nik didn't. It had snuck up on us and hardened into something else.

Nik signed up for food stamps. Of course I knew, and Nik knew, that wasn't the whole story. But still. Food stamps, don't kid yourself, they help and they don't.

When I was pregnant with Ada, they asked me if I wanted WIC coupons. (I don't remember what WIC stood for. Women in Calamity? Wombs in Crisis? Whiners in Christ?) They told me my income qualified me for WIC pre- and postnatal care and WIC essential food items. I used them for a long time. I got cheese and juice, and later, after she was born and I discovered that my postpartum migraine meds made it a problem to breastfeed, I used WIC for the very expensive formula Ada required. I needed the help. But the coupons were a pain. Each month you had to pick them up in person. You could only go to the supermarkets that accepted them. You could only buy certain things with them. And everyone in line saw you use them. And you knew whatever else you bought (God forbid you bought cigarettes or beer or even a candy bar), even though you paid your own money for it, would be scrutinized by everyone in line. It didn't have to go like that—but it did, and the message was clear to me. I used to drive all the way over to the west side so I could use the Albertson's there. I dreaded running into people I knew. First I had to get someone to open the locked case where the formula was kept. (I never asked why baby formula had to be kept in a locked case. I didn't want to know.) Then I felt helpless as I watched the checkout girl sigh when I showed her the coupons—using them was a complicated transaction involving signatures and product codes and manager approvals.

More than once I would drive out of my way, find the smallest line, go last, and then discreetly hand over the coupon to have the checkout girl call over the intercom loudspeaker for the manager and then wait, holding up the line as the girl held my coupons aloft.

Later, when I got health insurance through another state program, one that issued a regular insurance card that didn't identify how it was funded, I remember how the nurse at my doctor's office asked me, "WIC, right?" I said no, and I handed her my new insurance card, and she said, "Good for you!" with a big smile. I smiled back, because what else was I supposed to do? So the food stamps may not have been the whole story, but they certainly made up some significant chunk of the story.

"Did you find out about getting disability?"

He shook his head.

"What? Did you even ask them?"

"It takes ages and ages to get disability. I don't think I qualify, anyway."

"You didn't even ask, did you?" I said.

"Oh yeah, I did."

"What did they say?"

"ABAWD can GFH."

"What?"

"Able-bodied adult without dependents can go fuck himself."

"You have to apply, you really can't work."

Nik took my hand and squeezed it. I got the faintest whiff of bourbon. "Don't worry. I got it covered."

"How, just how, are you going to cover it?" I said. My mouth set, and I shook my head.

"I got it, you'll see."

"I'll tell you what you got, okay? I'm so goddamn sick of your 'handling' things. You don't handle anything, ever. You live in your fantasy world and it all costs me. It all will end up my problem. Like Mama, like your rent, like fucking everything. It is all on me."

Nik looked at me, not smiling. I knew I was going to regret it, but I glared at him, unmoved.

"I just can't do it all. Not anymore. It is too much."

Nik broke into a huge grin. "What, are you breaking up with me?"

I sighed.

"Because no one has ever broken up with me." He put an arm around me. "I get it, I understand. You are right. I'm sorry." I felt the tears, but that was no shock to him or me because I always cry over everything.

"I just worry about what will happen in the future. In the near future. We can't act like kids forever."

"Oh my God, you're right! We are all growed up! Holy crap, Dee Dee."

Okay, so he made me laugh about it, about my fear and my worry. But things couldn't and didn't stay the same. They got harder. It was getting harder all the time. All of this was much harder than it used to be. For me.

I measure the distance between things. Isn't that what memory is for? Isn't that what *this* is for?

APRIL 28

This day, this limping, awful day. Where to begin? The morning, of course. Recounting the beginning is easy—we have the actual film Ada made, and I don't have to remember anything; I have it on tape.

Ada was not going to make an invisible Maysles Brothers–type documentary. She wasn't going to pretend it was some objective version of reality. She would interact and ask questions. It was a film about her family, after all. She wanted to film me walking around Runyon Canyon, but I put the kibosh on that. I wanted to be a static talking head. They set up the camera, Ada asked me the questions and then urged me to talk and talk. She wanted hours. She had questions, but she didn't yet know where it would go. She was of the organic documentary theory that a pure, authentic narrative would emerge in the editing process after they waded through the footage.

(Insert here—somehow—the excerpted clip from *Garageland,* the movie.)

In the meantime, the transcript as I recall it:

I sat on a stool. Instead of using my pathetically suburban house as a backdrop, I was shot in an empty room with one of Nik's collages behind me. It was the one of him that was made by putting all nineteen covers of The Ontology of Worth *together. So this mosaic of Nik loomed over me, with one piece missing—the still, at the time of filming, unreleased* Volume 1. *(When I watched this part of the film a few days later, it reminded me of the brainwashing sequence from* The Manchurian Candidate, *where the main character sits in front of a huge playing card. What was his name? The character's name was Shaw. But I couldn't recall the actor. Then I remembered it was Laurence Harvey, of course. Beautiful, gay Laurence Harvey. Oh, and here is how I remembered his name: Laurence Harvey died at forty-seven from ~~suicide~~ stomach cancer. Or did I misremember that?)*

ME

Right. Is it okay if I drink coffee during this? Are we starting already? Okay.

ADA *(offscreen)*

Why don't you tell me, Ma, how Nik started making the Chronicles. Why did he?

ME

I guess it really started around '79 or '80. It coincided with his ending his band. 1979 was the last year Nik was actually in a band. The year of the big disappointment. I think it is fair to describe it as not entirely a surprise. Nik was faking it. I knew it, he knew it. He wasn't really interested in the punk or post-punk music scene that was exploding. He was too old, for one thing. Nik was twenty-five and everyone else was like seventeen. He was a poseur, as we used to say.

I took a sip of water. I paused for the effect of recollection.

It is important to understand what was going on in those days. After years of deadness, Los Angeles suddenly had this legitimate scene. Nik cut his hair super short. He knew what would work. No gigs unless you had that look. But already Nik betrayed himself with harmony and hooks. Why not? The Sex Pistols and the Clash had harmonies and hooks. Okay, you spat and you cursed, but it wasn't ever that far from the Beatles. What you couldn't do, though, ever, was play solos. No guitar pretension and no drum solos and no complications. Fine. But LA was not London. LA had to answer for the Eagles and Jackson Browne. LA had some issues in it. Somehow out of the good sun and the long days, LA felt a deep ugly rage. It was swollen with heroin and debauched wastedness. It was a badly stitched, angry-red, keltoid-scar rage. It was a self-scratched, blue-inked, infected-prison-tattoo rage. I understood, almost instantly, what that rage meant. I loved that rage, the anti-tan pasty look, the deliberately ugly. I understood how subversive ugly could be. We had a terrible hunger for the nasty, the horrible, the deformed.

ADA

So you were involved in the punk scene?

ME

Not really. I was also too old, for one thing. I would soon be pregnant with you. No—I was a veteran of pre-punk LA. We went to Rodney's English Disco and the Sugar Shack. That was an underage club. We used to take quaaludes in the parking lot because there was no drinking allowed. The glitter scene—we didn't call it glam then, we called it glitter—was all about looking good, looking sexy. So you are eighteen, on quaaludes and dressed like a whore—I don't have to explain that this often led to a less than fulfilling outcome for young women. By the time I was twenty-one, I was already bored of all of it.

Then I discovered Johnny Rotten. I first read about him in the *Melody Maker* and *New Musical Express.* I used to go to the Universal News stand on Las Palmas and get the British magazines—

(Ada later would insert a shot of Universal News as it looks today. It still has the sign in plastic blue sans serif letters on stained concrete.)

I would read about how the Sex Pistols cursed on TV. How they insulted the queen. How they put safety pins in their ears. How they vomited at the airport. And how they insulted their audience, told their audience they were being ripped off. The thing that really got me was the interviews I read. Johnny Rotten said rock and roll was boring. He said sex was boring. They wore zippered bondage pants, but they couldn't be bothered. I was like, yes! Not because I really thought sex was boring, but because I knew that was revolution. No one except us girls understood how subversive Johnny Rotten's anti-sex stance really was. So obnoxiously and unanswerably defiant, the perfect retort to any concern: *It's boring*. Even SEX bores us. I wondered why Rotten didn't attack the other rock-and-roll cliché and say drugs were boring? Still, rock and roll is like 90 percent sex, so the nihilism of Rotten's anti-sex stance cannot be exaggerated.

ADA

Do go on, Mom. We can always cut it out later.

ME

Right. Right. I had already wearied of even my own easy allure. I saw girls making their own T-shirts (because making your own was the thing). One girl I remember made a ripped white T-shirt that read: *No, I don't want to give you a blow job.* Girls shaved half their hair to make themselves look like Soo Catwoman, the Sex Pistols' girl sidekick. I even loved Sid Vicious's girlfriend, Nancy Spungen. She had a face like a wound. I loved her gobby big mouth, her lumpy thighs, her sallow bad skin.

I wasn't heavily into any scene; I had a job and everything. But I still walked around Melrose in my layers of pinned black clothes, steaming in the sun, and I would hear the Brentwood girls giggling and pointing their chins at me. I looked down on them. We all did. But even as we wanted that Nancy ugly, we thought we looked really good. There is no escape, finally, from it. I mean, we didn't really want to look bad, we just had this very contextual, specific aesthetic that was precious because it was only readable to those in the know. Who cared about anyone who didn't get it? Sure, we still gave blow jobs to boys, but only to certain boys, the right boys. The boys who got it.

ADA

Okay, but maybe you could get back to Nik?

ME

Right, I should get back to Nik. Around this time, Nik formed his band the Fakes. Nik had the sensibility down. And Nik had the look down. He was born to look pasty and skinny and angular. The look wasn't the problem. The sound, well, that was always the issue. Nik's other band, the Demonics, had a small following, they had some weird sonic experimentations. They veered into long, meandering songs. They were dark in an out-of-step kind of way. No one knew what to do with them.

Anyway, Nik invented the Fakes as the antidote to the darkness and oddness of the Demonics—the Fakes were a side band designed to play power pop and have fun. They came right at the moment when the nihilism of the punk scene had run its course and people were hungry for some simple rock pop, some harmonies, with a danceable beat as long as the band looked New and Cool. People could dance to the Fakes, and they became much more popular than the unclassifiable Demonics. Nik did it as a kind of lark. He did it as a kind of calculation.

ADA

But Nik's pop songs were always the best thing he did. The other projects don't age as well, don't you think?

ME

He doesn't feel that way. But he loved making fun pop songs and was very good at it.

ADA

What happened with the Fakes? With that sound, why didn't they make it?

ME

Well. They almost did.

ADA

What do you mean? I never knew that.

ME

I shouldn't have brought it up. It is a long sore story.

ADA

How come I never heard about it before? What happened?

ME

I don't even know what happened. You'll have to ask Nik. But he won't talk about it.

ADA

Well, can you tell me everything you do know?

ME

I can't. I would be guessing. You will just have to ask him.

ADA

You two never talked about it?

ME

We never did.

ADA

I don't believe it.

ME

It seemed almost rude, somehow. Like it violated the rules between us. We don't talk out everything. We keep a lot in the air between us. Why is this so important?

ADA

It's not, I just feel like it would explain a lot.

ME

I don't think it would explain much about Nik. At all. I think you are missing the point about Nik. Making it with his fake band? I don't think it was important. But you could make it seem that way if you wanted to.

Ada said nothing. She glared at me.

ME

I'm sorry.

ADA

Cut.

That was the end of my interview. I guess it didn't go so well. She took her two-person crew and went over to Nik's to do his interview. Wait until she tried to push him into her narrative suppositions, her easy causations, her inciting incidents, and her cinematic reductions. Her "editing later." Try it out on Uncle Nik.

I never get mad at Ada, so this feeling was new for me. I was mad, I could feel it. I resented her wanting to know everything. And to order it somehow. The truth is, although I never asked Nik about it, I also used to wonder what really had happened.

I had first glimpsed the way things were going when I

watched him play at the Fakes' first three gigs. By the second gig, all the little girls had come out. The underage girls from the Valley. It was like the word went out into the little-girl underground. The front of the stage was a sea of pogoing chicklets in miniskirts and golden perms. They wore lots of eyeliner and they gave their love to the boys on the stage. By the third gig, the Fakes were a hit, a sensation, albeit on an extremely local level. I'm not sure exactly how that happened. Had the Fakes been touted by a mention on KROQ? I don't remember the details. And Nik would never talk about it, no matter how drunk he was. I could, I guess, go back through the Chronicles, but of course that would not be an accurate rendering of history. Or, another way to put it, it would be an accurate rendering of how Nik viewed it, history put through the Nik-o-lyzer. In any case, as I recall it, this was the moment one of the pestilent pop impresarios appeared in Nik's life. Lee "Lux" Smith had long lurked at the periphery of the various Los Angeles scenes. I have sort of tracked him over the years. He always turned up in the margins, he always had his icky fingers in an anthology or a documentary. His mother was a famous actress—he worked out of her enormous Laurel Canyon mansion. He had the odor of privilege about him; he drove a pristine white 1966 Mustang convertible.

Lux started out as a songwriter. He penned a couple of hit singles for a sixties novelty group, the Ginger Jangles (yes, they had red hair). After that, Lee had attached to various marginal acts. One was a young whisper-voiced girl who was trying to do the Emmylou Harris/Gram Parsons southern angel stuff. She had long native-straight black hair and she sang her country pop without pedal steel guitar or anything too offensively country. She had some minor success and then quickly disappeared. Then there was Lee Lux's other protégé, an uncomfortably handsome singer from Canada who bleated out didactic political songs with acoustic accompaniment. Lux remade him as some kind of glitzed-out superstar and quickly got a record deal. Lux saw to it that they spent a lot of money, and the singer's first album had these huge, lush production numbers. He was hyped beyond belief, shoved on billboards, and seemed to be opening for everyone. But the hype didn't hit the right note for his still-earnest presentation. Or maybe he was too pretty or the timing was bad. His one and only record sank without a trace. You can still buy it on eBay for a chunk of money, perhaps if you are a collector of obscurities. Or a collector of artifacts of people who sell out for exactly nothing in return. But that sounds like a terrible, mean thing to collect.

One wonders, or at least I wonder, what happened to these people? Not the one-hit wonders but the no-hit wonders? Those actual people who became roadkill as the Lee Lux types move on. I can easily imagine the unreturned phone calls. The years when a second chance still feels within reach. But then what? I wonder, of course, because Nik is sort of one of them. Someone, somewhere, no doubt wonders what became of roadkill Nik. But it really pains me to think of him in this category. I shudder to think of him as a footnote in the documentary yet to be made about Lee Lux Smith. Which is one of the reasons why I thought Ada's idea for her movie wasn't so bad, despite my noncompliance. I really didn't want the smug opportunists, the people who dine off other people's lives, to tell all the stories.

After Lee Lux failed with the singer-songwriter, he let it be known he was looking for a new act.

The Fakes were not the ideal candidates for Lux. But he wanted to find a way into the new new thing. And one thing I have to concede: Lux did recognize how good Nik was and how timely the Fakes were. I remember being backstage and seeing him appear. He must have been in his mid-thirties then—he just looked old to me. He wore a sport coat over a T-shirt. He pushed the sleeves of the coat up his arms a little, which must have been his concession to the moment—he was, after all, all about concessions to the moment. But he still looked out of place with his uncommitted haircut that was short in the front and long in the back, and his iron, handsome jaw, and his way of smiling that felt moneyed and important. I watched him throw a friendly arm around Nik and whisper to him. Already he colluded, naturally he was on Nik's side. He knew things, he could grow and spin his indispensability in the course of a conversation. Nik waved me over. I remember exactly how it went down.

"Dee Dee, this is Lee Lux." Nik called me Dee Dee back then. Denise was only for serious moments and my mother. I held out my hand and gave him a cheeky sarcastic wink. At twenty-one I had somehow developed the manner of a drag queen. This was my version of punk attitude. He kissed my hand and I curtsied.

"Now, why isn't this creature in the band? You can stand behind a keyboard, can't you, darlin'?" Lee said. God, he really was a shameless sleazeball. He was so corny, it was almost fabulous, you know? Almost, but not at all, actually. Up close I could see he had a mouthful of gleaming straight teeth. From his mother, I couldn't help thinking. That is the thing about these sorts of people. They are quite charming, and shallow as it sounds, everyone likes some shiny teeth. (One other truly subversive thing about the Sex Pistols and the British punks: bad teeth. Bad smells, bad teeth, bad skin—this was the real stuff of rebellion. It didn't last long as an aesthetic. But wasn't it amazing for a moment?)

Nik and I went to Hamburger Hamlet on Sunset Boulevard with Lee Lux. The rest of the band was cordially not invited. That was the first sign, I think, that this guy was bad news. But we also already knew he was bad news. Everyone knew it—so you had your guard up. But Lux used that notoriety and made it work to his advantage.

He said, "You know me. Everyone knows me. I am the king opportunist. I am the ruthless man-eating star maker. Either get with me or get out of my way because I'm not nice."

We all laughed.

He said, "You can be nice. I can be the cutthroat. I have no qualms, none whatsoever, about doing what needs to be done. I am a shark, I am a piranha."

Nik chain-smoked. He didn't say anything at all, but he listened. I sipped a Coke. Lux bit into a hamburger. He said, "Tell me what you see for yourself. Where would you like to be in two years?" He pushed his french fries away from his burger and ignored them. Nik leaned his face wearily into his hand and looked around the restaurant. He said nothing, then started laughing. "Seriously," said Lux.

Nik shrugged. He said, "Look, you know, the Fakes are just

for fun. I have much better stuff than the Fakes." Lux nodded. He had finished every bite of his burger. I watched him very carefully—I ate nothing in those days. I wanted to be skeletal. But I was fascinated watching other humans eat.

Lux said, "The music is fine. I really like the music the way it is. The music is perfect. But maybe you don't need that cynical name . . ."

Nik laughed again. "Too cynical?" he said. "What name would you suggest?"

Lux gave up and finally popped two french fries in his mouth. "I don't know. Maybe the Real? Or the True?"

Nik shook his head. "Nope."

Lux shoved a few more french fries in his face. "Look, maybe not, but with the Real, say, you can be ironic to the new wave kids and sincere to the rest of the kids. You can have it both ways. If you want to be successful, you have to get things to work in many, many ways to many, many people." Nik didn't say anything, but I could tell he was considering it. We left that meeting, and I felt sure Nik wouldn't bother with Lux. And he never changed the name of the band, it was true. But it didn't go away. Lee Lux hovered around. He arranged opportunities for the Fakes without Nik asking for them. He was growing his indispensable qualities. Maybe Nik's ambivalence was a form of consent. Maybe there was a more formal agreement between them. I don't really know. But I do know Lux stuck around, fixated on the Fakes for a while. And he had a finger or two in the record deal that was offered to Nik in the summer of 1979.

Okay, the funny thing is I don't really know what went

wrong. I wasn't lying to Ada. I mean, Nik never explained it to me or anyone. More or less, a record deal with an actual major label, Sire, which was the Ramones' label, was in the offing. Then there was another label. And it all blew up. It was all on the verge, but another LA band, maybe the Dickies, their record had come out on a real label and it was a flop. Maybe that was part of it. But I also think—well, I know—that when it became clear he was not going with Lux, Lux helped blow things up. Lux was setting it up, and when Nik told Lux to fuck off, Lux may have sabotaged it. Then Nik was too tainted to get an independent label interested. So what Lux said was true—get with him or else. After that happened, Nik changed his life. Ada was right to an extent. That time, '79–'80, was a kind of turning point.

He broke up the Fakes. He broke up the Demonics. He stopped going out. I didn't see him for months. I was still living at home—I had just had Ada, and Mom was helping me. Nik had moved into his own apartment over the garage in Topanga Canyon. I didn't hear from him. I called a couple of times and spoke with him. I just thought he was depressed. He was going through that stage when you realize your youthful dreams are not panning out. I was going through my own version of that, reconciling myself to my new responsibilities. That was all normal. And, yeah, I thought Nik would get over it.

Then one day I get a call. Nik wants me to come over to hear his new record. Which is news to me, that he has one. But he had been recording this solo record. He did it all by himself with his four-track. It is a great record, introspective and with these very simple, understated, overdubbed harmonies. When I sat in his apartment and heard it, I was so moved. Then he said, "Do you want to read the reviews?"

I said, "Uh, yeah, sure." He pulled out the Chronicles. The precursor to the Chronicles had begun years before. It was simply a scrapbook of Nik's real life. His music life, which was his whole life. He pasted in flyers from gigs, photos, capsule mentions in the paper, that sort of thing. He put in pages announcing the records and detailed the track listings. He had been making his own records for years. But this was the first time Nik put a fake review in his Chronicles.

***LA WEEKLY*, August 1, 1981**
Nik Worth Goes Solo
by Stiv Stereo

Nik Worth's brilliant post-punk band, the Fakes, made a huge splash this year with their debut album, *Here Come Your Fakes.* Nik Worth, their laconic lead singer, has come out with a self-produced solo album on the heels of that success, entitled *Meet Me at the Movies.* This album, made entirely by Worth in his home studio, is a completely different affair. Where the power pop effervescence of a single like "Gold Girls" on *Here Come Your Fakes* made it irresistible on the dance floor, Worth is after a darker, more experimental effect in this solo effort. He initiates acoustic fragments of songs, minor and even elegiac, and then segues into other, more complex songs like "Take Me Back" and "Sweep Song." Toward the end of the record there is even a music-only reprise of the lovely "Sweep Song" titled "Singalong Sweep Song." The sort-of song cycle seems to waiver from quiet to intense, and then builds to what can only be described as an old-fashioned power ballad, "(I'll Wait) All of My Life." This song is an instant classic, the kind of song no one writes anymore. It features a slow build, a quiet intro on the in verse, and then a commanding rising riff, and at last a restrained but undeniable guitar solo, bringing the power home. Will the Fakes fans dig this throwback to the slower days of pop? With a great cover shot of a decidedly brooding Worth and a lyric sheet that steers well clear of the sentimental, I think they will. A–

I did not yet realize how elaborate this new phase would get. He recorded more music, and then he wrote in the Chronicles about the music. Sometimes they were good reviews. Sometimes they were pans. From this point on, his real life and his life as recorded in the Chronicles diverged.

After filming, I spent the afternoon at my mother's. It was blessedly uneventful. As I was leaving, she told me that Nik had been to see her. Funny he went to see her without mentioning it to me.

I got into my car. I couldn't wait to get home, get in my bathrobe, eat my dinner, watch something stupid on TV. It was good that he was stepping up without my arranging it. Usually I would have to push him to see her. He avoided it except on birthdays and holidays. He would say it was difficult for him to see her "like this." Especially, somehow, for him. I know how he justified it: he thought his seeing Mom like this cost him more than it cost me. "You are better at taking care of people than I am, let's face it," he said. As if it were some kind of compliment. I muttered as I drove. Yeah, he is so fucking sensitive, and I am so strong. Nothing is difficult for me, right? The really irritating part, of course, was that my mother adored Nik. She wouldn't complain about his not visiting, because even in her diminished state she was protecting him. She loved me, truly, and let me look after her, but she adored Nik, and still looked out for him. I glanced in the rearview and caught a glimpse of something most unbecoming. I bared my teeth at myself and actually said, "Grrrr." It didn't make how I felt any more becoming. But it melted my self-pity into self-loathing, which was better somehow.

I got home exhausted and starving. I made a salad. I tore off a heel of bread and balanced it on the edge of the plate. I poured a glass of wine. It was dark and quiet. I clicked on the television to see what was happening in the real world.

BREAKING EVENT #5

All they showed was the one photo. The man standing on the box. That picture was it. It had the weird KKK silhouette of the pointy hat and the cloak. It had the imitation-of-Christ pose. Then you noticed the wires coming from the hands, the bare feet. I watched in a daze while vaguely hearing what the people were saying—they said the word *shocking*, they struggled to find a tone that worked. This time it was easy to ignore the stream of news that ran across the bottom of the screen. I ended up at my computer, at a magazine's website. Eleven images had been posted.

At first, all I could see were the bodies against the cement and the plastic. Then the people in the bright blue rubber gloves and the khaki uniforms. I felt an animal fear, a queasy medical-experiment fear as familiar objects became dislocated and warped.

I looked at these naked bodies. With the plastic hoods, they all looked alike: ordinary human bodies, fragile at the knees and ankles and wrists. Their dusty bare feet struggled to hold their poses. The skin was pale under the Powershot—or maybe the Sureshot—flash. Their genitals were pixelated out by the magazine's editors. But the faces of the soldiers were clearly visible. They looked young. They looked casual and slightly bored. The corridors and cells were cement painted a high-gloss industrial beige or yellow. The flash bounced off the walls and made them glisten. The floor looked wet from seeped-in moisture. The naked men lay or were laid on it. What was I supposed to do with these images?

I kept looking. But although I felt the raw indecency of it, although I could feel my heart pounding and my mouth get dry—actual autonomic nerve reactions to panic, an effect felt at a basal level, related somehow to my self-protection—my reaction was merely that: revulsion. Otherwise my engagement was intellectual, not emotional. It hit my stomach and my head. I couldn't make emotional sense out of it.

I kept on looking.

Something held me. It wasn't the victims, the masked heap of naked men. I already knew about that. It was the young soldiers. I could see—I quickly came to understand—that the soldiers had posed and arranged these photos. They were not surreptitious shots but a little show created by them. One soldier in particular kept turning up, a tiny young woman who smiled as she posed for the camera. Her cheer among the faceless bodies broke through the noise, all right. The experience of seeing these photographs was overwhelming, but I could begin to locate it, feel it, in this girl's face.

MAY 10 INTO EARLY MAY 11

For the past week, I had watched the news whenever I was home. I hardly thought about my own life at all. The story did not disappear—it seemed to gather momentum, it seemed to be getting worse. I followed the coverage closely, what the major-general said, what the secretary of defense said. The president spoke about the "shameful and appalling acts." I simultaneously searched around the web to the rest of the world. I went to sites based in Jordan and the United Arab Emirates, sites with Arabic writing I couldn't read but lots of photos I could see. These photographs were everywhere.

When I went to bed, I was totally exhausted and not at all able to sleep. I turned the television back on. I clicked through to the late-night shows. People were making jokes about the young women in the photos, particularly the one smiling girl's pointing and thumbs-up in front of the naked and hooded prisoners. She was everywhere.

I tried to imagine her growing up in West Virginia. Being a not very special girl and growing up in a trailer park. I could see the bad sex at an early age after drinking the bad beer. I could see the high school guidance counselor and the long drab future. Then the recruiter and a chance to leave. You either joined up or stayed home and got pregnant. I would have joined up, too, I think. But then what? I didn't want to think any more about this girl, but I wanted to know, after the bad sex and the shit school and the recruiter, then what happened to her?

The story of these photos and this girl was banner news for the moment. But I knew she and the whole story would be put aside, even though it was an election year. The president had already denounced her, significant people had drawn the line, and the soldiers would be charged as the sick aberrations we all knew they were. But even if that were true—and it was difficult for anyone to believe that this wasn't a typical part of a much bigger picture—it still didn't mean what they wanted it to mean.

I flipped through the channels. I stopped at an in-progress episode of a police drama. My eyes were stinging from lack of sleep, but my mind jig-jagged, and I knew the best I could hope for was that this show would bore me into a stupor on the couch and I could click off the TV and fall asleep.

No matter what I watched, I couldn't be distracted from the young soldier. I couldn't figure her out. She eluded any explanations. Was she trying to fit in and be tough? Was she told that she had to do this or else? Was she just stupid, a damaged antisocial product of fetal alcohol syndrome or malnourishment in infanthood? I could only come up with a cliché sense of her that was too general to mean anything. It wasn't just the smile on her face that unnerved, it was the repetition and the need to photograph and the easy indifference. The porn aesthetic that people slipped into and what it meant about the kind of lives they had lived. Waiting, talking about nothing, waiting. Corn slapped out of a can. Pimples and bruises on pale white skin. All the smells of close quarters and the inadequate solace of another cigarette. But still.

Then I read somewhere, on some blog or newspaper website, that this girl, this notorious United States Army soldier, longed to be a storm chaser. She dreamed of following cyclones and filming hurricanes when they make landfall. I was falling asleep, and I found some release in that phrase, *make landfall,* and I liked the sound and feel of those words, *hurricane* and *cyclone,* they made the world feel human-sized again, and I was nearly asleep at last—

And it hit me. I realized it, and the realization blew hurricanes and cyclones and horrible photographs and sleep right out of my mind. Of course: Nik's health, Tommy's death, visiting our mother. The hyperordered state of his apartment. And the last album in the twenty volumes of *The Ontology of Worth* being finished and released for his upcoming fiftieth birthday. *I've got it all under control.*

I sat up. I knew what he was planning to do, and I knew it absolutely.

How could I be so thick? How could I be so careless? I looked at my watch: 3:58. I couldn't call him now. The next morning, after a few hours of sleep on the couch, I drank coffee and thought of what I should do. I looked at my email. I called Nik and told him I wanted to come over after work. He said he had a shift that night and I could come see him at the bar.

MAY 11

Nik didn't hear me come in. He was sitting on a stool. He hunched over a paperback book he had pinned to the bartop with a splayed hand. He held a cigarette with the other hand. I stood and looked at him for a second, my big brother. His hair fell down in his eyes. He frowned a little and took a drag. He stamped out the cigarette in an ashtray, flipped the book cover-side up (Hermann Hesse's *The Glass Bead Game*), and made circle motions with his shoulders as he moved his head from side to side. At last he saw me.

"Hey!" I said. He waved me over.

"Hiya," he said, and I leaned over the bar and gave him a kiss. I could smell cigarettes, of course, and a citrus oversmell that must have been his shampoo or hair gel. No bourbon this time. Neither he nor I would mention our last fight. Mostly because our fights consisted of me freaking out over something and him placating me until it blew over. It was just the way it went with us, the way it always was. He took out a bottle of the amber beer I usually have when I come in. I nodded. Every gesture of his seemed at least darkly meaningful if not downright cryptic.

"I'm glad to see you. It's been dead and I'm falling asleep here." He turned to the stereo and punched up a new song. It was some ultrafamiliar sixties rhythm and blues, but much more rhythm than blues. The kind of music that made you want to move against your will, as if it plugged in to some preconscious and involuntary need for beat and repetition. It did not mirror the moment for me.

"Can you turn that down? A little?"

Nik shrugged and turned it down.

"What's going on?"

"Nothing," I said, smiling. I looked in his eyes. He betrayed nothing. "How are you feeling? How's your foot?"

"I'm okay, actually pretty good," he said. Nik smiled. He had, considering our haphazard visits to the dentist as children and his lifetime devotion to smoking, these straight white teeth, and his smile still made him look almost boyish. I have decent teeth, but I have a narrow and strictly horizontal smile that makes my lips turn knife-blade thin and my eyelids pooch into little pillows of flesh. I often used to wonder what it would be like to go through life with a flashy Nik-type smile. "What?" he said.

"I was thinking something, I have this idea," I said.

"Yeah?"

"Maybe you could . . . I think I need some help with my mortgage," I said.

"Oh yeah?"

"Yes, I need to get a roommate," I said.

"A roommate? Really? What about Thomas Kinkade?" Nik said, smirking now.

I shook my head. "Jay and I are not about to live together. No! I just met him, c'mon," I said. I took a swig of beer. No way would he go for this, or make this easy, but I had to try it and see. "I was thinking you have had difficulty paying your rent. You could move in to my place. You could have the guest room, and you could turn the garage into your studio." There, I had offered it. It was possible—I did have a guest room, which I used hardly ever.

Nik shook his head and smiled again, but this time it was one of his brow-furrowed wincing smiles with a sigh blown through it, clearly meaning *are you bat-shit out of your mind?* I looked around the room. Nobody else was in the bar. It was early. He waved a hand at me.

"What?" I said.

"Jesus, I don't want to live with you, are you fucking kidding? You really are so funny. You don't want to live with me either, trust me." Which was totally true, I did not want him to smoke in my house or to be there when I got home. I did not want him to play music all the time and I didn't want to find out how much he really drank. I hadn't lived with Nik since I was seventeen. I had no idea what he was really like, his toothpaste and his coffee and his dirty laundry. But.

"Well, I could use the company and the help. So consider it. For my sake." He patted me on the head like I was an imbecile. He held up another bottle of beer and waved it at me. I shook my head no. I sat and picked at the label of my nearly empty beer bottle. I couldn't leave yet. He thought I was lonely, that that was what this was about, and I could tell he felt sorry for me even though he said nothing. He smiled at me, and it had his special reluctant sister-pity in it. He hadn't guessed my motives, not yet.

"Ada's coming back to town soon?"

"Ada is coming this weekend," I said.

"So I guess Ada's making me a movie star," he said.

"Yes, yes. Good. It is all happening. How do you feel about it?"

He shrugged. "It's fine with me. It's not like I'm gonna say no." He took a sip from a beer bottle he kept down below and out of sight; he must have kept it in the liquor speed rack. "She won't actually finish it, don't you think?"

"I don't know. Ada is very determined. I wouldn't underestimate her. She raised enough money to get this far." Maybe, just maybe, he wasn't going to do what I feared. Maybe I had it all wrong. He was thinking about the future, wasn't he? The movie was a good thing. I realized then I should have been pushing the movie, not resisting it. "You never know, Nik, documentaries are big now. She could get HBO to back it. You could get discovered at fifty. At the very least you could get a label interested in releasing your music."

"C'mon. It won't really be about the music. It will be about 'my freaky uncle.' That's how it will go."

I shook my head. He took another swig off his beer bottle.

"That's all right. I don't mind. Don't get me wrong. I like the attention. I'll take what I can get at this point. Hell, I'll be the next Henry Darger. Do you remember how that movie ended? The outsider artist dies and the whole world discovers he was secretly a genius. Can you imagine how much his estate must be worth now?"

Now it was my turn to do my *are you crazy* head shake at him. "What are you talking about?"

"I'm just shooting my mouth off. You know me."

I did know him, didn't I?

MAY 23

I know Ada did her last interview with Nik this day. I haven't seen the interview yet. It wasn't strictly part of his Chronicles because it was about the Chronicles, and the Chronicles don't exist in the Chronicles, of course. So Ada's movie fits into *my* chronicles, the fact-based ones. I will have to, at some point very soon, watch it, and I will have to include it to give a full accounting.

May 23; we were getting very close.

After Ada interviewed Nik, both of them came over, and we all drove to my mother's apartment. Nik's second visit with her in a week. My mother greeted us with a huge grin. I brought food for dinner, and we all sat around the table and ate.

"This chicken is delicious," my mother said. Nik didn't eat, but sipped at a beer.

"Yes, it's great," he said. He watched her as she ate. I felt relief that she seemed to be her old self today. As if I needed her to put on a good show for Nik. He looked intently at our mother while I looked intently at him.

"How did the filming go?" I asked.

"Excellent. We may have to do some more. But with the first interview, it was a good start. Right?" Ada said. When she was serious, she looked like me. The worried eyebrows and the way her fingers rubbed at her lips.

"Yes, it was fun," Nik said.

"What's next?" I said.

"*The Ontology of Worth: Volume 1,* release party. It will be released on Nik's birthday next week. We will film the party. Nik will perform for the first time in thirty years. Then maybe we need to schedule one more interview."

"Really?" I said.

"A short acoustic set, that's all."

"Nik will be fifty. My word," my mother said. We all turned to her.

"Why, yes, absolutely he will be fifty," I said. How did she remember that? One day she is paranoid and erratic, the next day she is fine. I did, however, find a melted pint of ice cream in the cupboard. I grabbed it and quickly threw it away. I discreetly scoured the refrigerator for anything moldy that could make her sick.

"Did Leslie come by this morning?" I said.

"Yes, she did. I have to tell you, though," she said. Her eyes darkened and she pursed her lips. The lipstick was a little smeared, I noticed that now.

"What?" I said.

"She's stealing from me," she said. I shook my head. "She is. I had twenty dollars in my bag, and after she left, I couldn't find it."

"Ma, Leslie didn't take it, I promise you. You misplaced it." I caught Nik and Ada exchanging a look.

"It wasn't the first time, I didn't want to upset you, but she steals and she's terrible." My mother looked suddenly like a child, pouting and miserable. Of course it felt true to her.

"Mama, it is just your diabetes meds are making you paranoid. Leslie's good." I squeezed my mother's hand. I had to blame everything on the diabetes. That didn't sound as scary to either of us, and maybe it would make her less willing to try and sneak sweets. Her hand squeezed mine. I put my other hand on top of hers and stroked it lightly. She seemed to relax slightly. I held her hand, and she didn't pull back. It made sense. We started out with all this body intimacy when I was a baby and then a child. After that there were years when we hardly touched. We would give a hug or a kiss on the cheek, but it would be perfunctory. We would already be pulling away as we did it. It was just how adults behave. And now we were hugging, holding hands. I helped her at the doctor, I did her nails for her, I knew all about her body. It made sense—we retreated from the mind. The body remained. We lost the memories, and so the past collapsed and disappeared. We were back to the intimacy of our two bodies. And I realized the intimacy was never gone, not completely. It hummed just below our surfaces, held down by our array of vanities and privacies. It felt very simple, and very comforting, that our bodies get returned to each other in the end. It was almost as if the mind has to disappear to get us back to the elemental. To our pure mother-daughter love. It felt better when I thought of it like this, when I felt how good my touch made her feel. How it eased her fears.

When I think of my family, I think that our history really lives in our bodies. The mind distorts and fails, but the body endures until it doesn't, and up until that moment it held it all. I knew that when she died, it would be her body I would remember, her physical presence, and to recall any part of her body—her smell, her hair—would make me weep and grieve for her.

My father, from time to time, used to play piano in nightclubs and lounges. Nik remembers sitting under a grand piano while my father played. It was at some corny piano bar. I don't remember any of that. I don't even remember a single conversation I had with my father. I do remember, however, walking behind him on the street. He reached his hand back and opened it, then closed it and opened it without looking around for me. I ran up and pressed my palm into his palm. He closed his hand gently over mine, squeezed it. I remember how large his hand was, and how warm and heavy it felt.

I still have a photo of my father in my bedroom. It is his high school graduation picture. It is a black-and-white photo that has been painted with color, which is what they used to do to formal portraits. So it looks almost like a painting, or like a ghost. He looks young and handsome, a heavier version of Nik. But it doesn't remind me of him, really.

Occasionally—maybe three times it has happened—I get a sense of my father from other men. When I walk behind a certain kind of man in the street. It happened to me in New York City once. I was in a crowd and a man moved right in front of me. He brushed past me. He was wearing an overcoat. And because of his height, or maybe the way he carried himself, the way he walked, or the way his hair met the back of his collar. Or how his hand looked as he held his briefcase—something brought back my father. A deep, intimate body memory came over me; I could see him—somewhat—but I could feel him, or recall feeling him, completely. I glimpsed this stranger through the crowd and I startled. A flood of recognition and longing. I hurried after him, even tried to catch up. And then he turned slightly and I saw his face. I felt, ridiculously, real disappointment when I realized he was not my father. He did not look at all like my father. The incident didn't make me sad, though, it made me remember my father in ways a picture never could. I felt the memory of my father on my body, the way you feel a breeze or the heat of the sun. He did not feel—and so was not—entirely lost to me. Inside, beyond my recall of events and dates and talk, there was this hot-wired memory of his body. I know now how much all of us live in these body places. Your experiences, the hard-felt ones, don't fade. They are written forever in your flesh, your nerves, your fingertips.

MAY 25, 26, 27

Nik turned fifty. We met at Nik's apartment to celebrate. Ada brought her cameraman. I brought a cake and an envelope with a thousand dollars in it (borrowed at 18 percent interest). Ada had wanted a record release party and a concert, but Nik finally refused. It was just Ada and her cameraman, Nik, and me. I took this as an encouraging sign—no dramatic farewells. Nik handed us each a copy of *The Ontology of Worth: Volume 1*.

Ada held it up for the camera. I looked at the cardboard double CD case. I handed it back to Nik.

"What?" he said.

"Autograph, of course."

Nik smiled and took a marker to the inside of the gatefold. "That will be worth big money someday," he said with a wink. "The worth of Worth."

"Sounds like your next album title," I said. He put his finger to his nose to indicate *right on the nose* and smiled at me. Ada filmed us and we pretended she wasn't.

"Do you want to sing a couple of songs from the CD?" Ada said.

Nik picked up his guitar. "No, that would be kind of difficult. But since it is my birthday, I will perform something for you.

One song. An oldie." He sat on the edge of his couch. He started a slow, acoustic rendition of his teenage "hit" "Versions of Me." He closed his eyes, and he stretched the song, pulled it down low until his boy anthem of alienation turned into something else. It turned serious, slow, the declarations made wise and ironic; a reprise that made his age suit him for a moment.

When he finished, he looked up at me and I sniffed. "It's not a sad song," he said.

"But you made it sound—you changed it."

"Phrasing. It is all in the phrasing." Nik winked at me. No meaningful stares, no dark hints at all. He was happy, almost cheerful, for the rest of the night. Still, deep down, I knew what was coming.

After watching Nik drink many—closing on three—bottles of wine (with only a little help from me and Ada) and smoke many cigarettes, Ada and her cameraman cleared out to attend a friend's party in Santa Monica. I cleaned up and did the dishes. Nik watched me. After I finished, I sat down on the couch.

"Are you staying?" he said.

"I might. Is that okay?" He shrugged. He looked a little drunk and haggard. However, he spoke with precise sobriety. I wonder what it felt like to be him. Did he never actually get drunk? Is that why he drank so much? He lay back on the other end of the couch and stared at the ceiling.

"How does it feel to turn fifty?"

"Oh for God's sake."

"Sorry."

He got up and went into the bathroom. I could see a volume of his Chronicles sitting on his desk. I don't know why I was sneaking, but I thought I should look at them while I had the chance. I opened the neat, thick binder. I opened it to the end, to the last page inserted. Then I read what was typed on white paper and pasted in:

Nik Worth, Pop Star Turned Eccentric Innovator, Dies at 50

It was unfinished, just a headline. I heard him washing his hands. I closed the book and I sat back down on the couch. I rubbed my finger back and forth across my lower lip. I was at a loss. Nik came out of the bathroom.

"Hey, you gotta go. I'm beat," he said.

"Okay, but maybe you can make me some coffee? It is a long drive home." There was a near-catch in my voice.

"You should go now."

"Okay." I got up, then I sat back down. He exhaled noisily. I was really pissing him off. "Here's how it is," I said. "I'm scared. I'm worried something really bad is happening."

Nik shook his head. "You don't need to worry about me. It doesn't do a body any good."

"You're not going to do anything dramatic, right?"

"Denise, I'm fine, okay? Just because I turned fifty doesn't mean I'm going to off myself, you know?"

I nodded, unconvinced.

"You are making an error in your calculus of causality. You are misreading the signs. Seriously. Like the man said, the correlative is not the cause."

I started crying again. He went to the door and opened it. I continued to sit.

"I'm too tired to reassure you or explain things to you tonight. You are just going to have to trust me. Now please get the fuck out so I can go to bed."

"Okay, okay." I got up and left. And the next morning I called him.

"Still here," he answered the phone.

I laughed. "You are such an ass," I said.

"Yeah."

I stopped by his work on my way home (of course it wasn't vaguely on my way home). He smiled and waved me over. He had a few customers drinking at the bar. I sat at the end by the service station. He pointed a beer bottle at me and I nodded.

"How's it going?"

"Better," I said.

He looked over his shoulder at his customers and then looked at me. "Sorry I was such a dick last night."

I shook my head. "Let's forget all about that."

Nik nodded, and then leaned in over the bar toward me. It felt so intimate, I laughed.

"I mean, I feel the love, you know? I just want you to know that, all right?" he said.

"Okay," I said.

"You are the only one who ever really got me, you know? Of course you know." Then he held up a hand and limped down the bar, replacing beers and making change. He was starting to get busy. I finished my beer and stood up to leave. I waved at him. He walked over to my end of the bar and leaned to kiss my cheek.

"Goodbye," he said.

"Good night," I said. And I left.

There it was, the terrible decision I have to live with. I left him there, we said goodbye. I knew I might not see him again. But I had some very good reasons, reasons only a sister could understand. I knew that I could not stop him. But that wasn't it. I could have decided not to leave. I could have begged him, told him I couldn't live without him in my life. That wasn't it.

I didn't stop him. I admit it; I did not. And it wasn't just because I loved him so much I would give him up if I had to. If that was what he required for himself. I would support his decision, which I knew was not made lightly, but was planned in advance and gave him satisfaction. Although that is all true, that is not why I left him to his plan that night. I left him to it because I knew something, something true. Something maybe only I knew. He would go and I would stay. I would stay and watch as my life wound down. I would watch the decay and the quiet. I would endure the dregs and the hangover. I would stay till the end, to the slow slipping and gradual dropping away of my life. This was what I did: I endured. Nik would leave, and I would endure. It was always going to be this way. I knew it all along, didn't I? When I left, I felt liberated and even happy. He was done, and on his own terms, which was the only thing important to him. I would stay, waiting for the terms to unfold around me. That's the price you pay for staying around. That was okay for me, but it wouldn't do for him.

I'm not sure I really believe that, but at the time, for that moment when I left the bar, and for my drive home, this idea about him and about us was right. Maybe no one else would get it, but leaving him gave me a feeling of love and comfort. It felt generous, even if no one else would ever understand how.

I arrived at my home. I didn't watch the news or a movie. I called Ada. I emailed Jay. I took a lovely sky-blue pill, went to bed, and right away fell into a deep sleep.

MAY 28

I woke up at five a.m. in a panic. I got out of bed, and I knew something dreadful had happened. I called Nik and got no answer. I pulled on some clothes and rushed to my car. I considered calling the paramedics. But I didn't. I knew it would be too late. It didn't feel right or good anymore. I had made a mistake.

I opened my window and let hot dusty air blow through the car. I went over the speed limit. There was no one else on the freeway, there was only a dusty hazy hint of dawn light behind the mountains, and I imagined finding my brother. I imagined his body, cold and disturbed and pale, splayed across his bed. I had no doubt it would be pills. I knew he wouldn't hang himself or shoot himself. He would go using all of his hard-earned pharmaceutical skills, and for this I should be grateful. He probably knew exactly how to manage it without vomiting, some precise combination of barbiturates, alcohol, and a prescription-grade anti-emetic.

I would be able to handle seeing his body, wouldn't I? I could handle seeing it if he looked asleep, but I couldn't see it violated or messy. I just couldn't.

But my God, it wasn't just that. He had always accompanied

me, my entire life. I had no idea how to get on with it without him there, a constant steady presence. All I would have of him is memory, and that would never do me any good. That was no comfort. That was meager and not enough.

What have I done?

I looked up and I had pulled into his driveway. I forgot how to turn off my car, I stared dumbly at the ignition key in my hand after I finally pulled it out of the lock. I got out, I stumbled over something. I was still wearing my slippers. I felt a lack of breath that frightened me. I stopped and made myself breathe in and then out. I walked up the old wood steps, my hands trembling as I reached for the doorbell. My eyes flooded. I pushed the bell, heard the double cheerful chime, and waited. I peered through the window by the door, but the curtains were pulled closed and I couldn't see inside. I tried the knob. The door was unlocked. I opened the door, and I thought I might faint. I would faint. Maybe, just maybe, I would find him asleep, and everything would be okay. He would yell at me for waking him up, and I would confess how stupid I was. I walked into the room.

Nik was not in his bed.

He wasn't in the bathroom. Nik was not on his couch or down the trapdoor in his studio. I ran outside and looked for his car. I hadn't noticed when I came in, but his car was gone. I went back inside, then back outside, calling his name into the morning air.

The apartment was in perfect order. But now I did notice his guitars were missing except the one old one, the Orlando. Other things might be gone as well, I couldn't piece it all together yet.

And set out, displayed more or less, were the Chronicles, wide open on the desk. Waiting for me. On the open page was Nik's obituary:

Nik Worth, Rock Star Turned Eccentric Innovator, Dies at 50

Nik Worth, the eccentric genius and reclusive oddity, died yesterday of an apparent suicide. He was found unconscious at his home by his sister, Denise Kranis. No note was found at the scene, although his sister said, "He killed himself."

Dr. Mark Farmer, the LA County coroner, said preliminary autopsy findings indicated a drug overdose. The sheriff's department found bottles of the prescription drugs Nembutal and Anzemet by the bed, as well as a half-empty bottle of vodka.

Mr. Worth was born in 1956 as Nikolas Kranis. His father died when he was 11, and his mother has been sick in recent years. The family was poor, but Worth always felt he was well taken care of. He attended Hollywood High, and then, after a still-sealed conflict with the authorities, was expelled. He eventually graduated from Fairfax High School. He never attended college. It was at Hollywood High that he met the bandmates who would become his multi-platinum band, the Demonics. The Demonics pioneered a hard-edged post-glam art-rock sound that changed the course of popular music.

Mr. Worth's other band, the Fakes, followed the Demonics. The Fakes had a more pure pop sound, and they dominated the charts for much of the early eighties: *Meet the Fakes, Here Are Your Fakes,* and later, *Take Me Home and Make Me Fake It* all made number one in the US and the UK.

In 1980, Nik Worth was injured in a motorcycle accident.

It was then he began his long anti-pop project, *The Ontology of Worth,* a twenty-volume music experiment. Some thought it was brilliant, others referred to it as "Worth's Folly." Even admirers viewed it as self-indulgent. In response to the many parodies created about his later work, Worth only said, "Every man's life is an answer to the questions he asks," apparently quoting, inaccurately, Emerson.

In later years, Worth dropped from sight. Rumors abounded that his health, both mental and physical, was failing. He kept putting out the albums for his *Ontology* project, and he maintained a devoted but much smaller following. From time to time he put out a new Fakes record—recordings now made entirely by him in his home studio. The Fakes albums always sold well. But he stopped touring, and seldom left his "hermitage" near the Pacific Ocean, a large house on Skyline Drive in Topanga Canyon. According to friends, he never stopped working, recording, and writing. Many people speculate that there could be much more music still in the vaults at Skyline Drive.

Worth is survived by his mother, Ella Kranis, his sister, Denise Kranis, and his niece, Ada Vogel. In lieu of flowers, Denise Kranis requests donations be made in Worth's memory to the ASPCA, his favorite charity.

His obituary felt oddly perfunctory to me, as though Nik found the execution wasn't as fun as the idea of writing his own obituary, but I must confess some pleasure at guessing right about the drugs, even if I (thankfully) got life in the Chronicles confused with real life.

I think it is funny, and no doubt not at all lost on Nik, that in the end, his life in the Chronicles wasn't all that different from his real life. In some ways it was worse, and in other ways it was exactly the same. Not a fantasy perfect life at all, just a different life, perhaps a more artful life. But in the Chronicles he wasn't the author of the Chronicles, which was arguably the thing he had grown to be proudest of as time went by.

I was giddy with relief. I don't know why I didn't think he hadn't just gone off somewhere to kill himself, but I didn't. He was right. I hadn't read the signs right. I didn't guess he would just leave. And leaving seemed much, much better to me that morning. At first I was joyful.

On the next page was the odd fake letter from me to Ada. Was I supposed to discern clues here? I got some of the jokes in the obit. (Skyline Drive was Neil Young's address in Topanga, the opening lines were nearly verbatim from Elvis's *New York Times* obituary. No doubt there were other little jokes embedded that I would figure out later.) But there wasn't a note, an explanation, a letter to me of any kind. All I knew was that he left, and I knew he wasn't coming back. He was gone, and I didn't see it coming. It began to upset me. I had misread him, and that was hard to take. And so I sat down to figure it out, moment by moment, or at least remembered moment by remembered moment. I took his invitation, and, inadequate as I was to the task, I wrote it all out.

Denise put down her pen. The sun was setting again. But it was finished, she had inched her way back to this exact moment.

She desperately needed to sleep. But first, Ada. She finally called her and told her what had happened.

"What makes you think he is really gone for good?" she said. Denise said nothing. "Did you phone the police yet?"

"No. I should file a missing person report, right?"

"Yes, as soon as possible."

"Can you please help me with that?" Denise said. "I've been up for two days. I don't feel well."

"Of course. Poor Mama. I will come over. Just rest if you can. I will be there soon and I will take care of everything."

"Thanks, honey."

"He'll turn up, I bet."

"No, I don't believe he will." There was a pause. Denise could hear Ada exhale smoke.

"What will you do without Nik?"

"I'm going to lie down."

Denise hung up the phone. She looked around the room. Nik's bed was neatly made. Clean sheets just for her, no doubt. She pulled back the covers and crawled in. She held one of the pillows in her arms. She pushed her face into it. She lay on her side and pressed her face into Nik's pillow until she fell asleep.

When Denise woke up, it was dark out and Ada was in the room. She was hunched over the desk, looking at Nik's Chronicles. Denise sat up and rubbed her puffy face. She had been sleeping deeply, and it took her a moment to remember what had happened, where she was, and why Ada was there. Why Denise was there. Why. Ada came over to her and put her arms around her.

"How are you doing?" Denise said. Ada looked weepy and leaned in to her mother.

"How can you be so sure he isn't coming back?" Ada said. "I know, you just know and it is, whatever, a thing between a brother and a sister, or at least between you and Nik. You then must have a clue where he went?"

Denise shook her head. "I really don't. He took some of his guitars, he took, from what I can tell, some clothes. He took his car. But other than that, he left everything behind. All his Chronicles? His records? I don't get it. He doesn't have money. Wait—he has some money. I gave him a little money. I don't know—it is possible he went off to—" Denise looked around. "I don't know."

Ada made the call to the police. They would have to go in to file a missing person report. Ada said she could tell the police were not much invested in this missing person—he was in the willful-disappearance category, what they called a Voluntary Missing Adult. Which happens all the time, wives and mothers and daughters (and sisters) left by men who just want to disappear. They said people often return within a week or two. They also said she should get Nik's dentist to send over his dental records. Denise was nearly delirious. She got stuck, for some reason, on why your teeth were your body's only distinguishing feature, then she figured it out, and then she felt worse.

Denise didn't want to leave Nik's place, but Ada insisted they go back to Denise's house. Denise took a bath and Ada made some dinner. Denise responded to emails and called her boss. Tomorrow she would have to go to work, go to the police, and see her mother. She made a plan for the day. Ada stayed over. She would extend her trip for a few weeks.

"I'd like to finish my film," she said. Denise sighed. "I don't think I am being crass. I think more than ever Nik would want it finished."

"Well, he gave you an ending, didn't he?"

"I just think he left behind everything for a reason. So I want to go and explore his archives. I want to film the details of his collection of stuff. I want to record the handmade labels, the collages, the intricate systems of order and reference. It would be so great."

"I don't think I like that idea. I don't think you should go through his stuff."

"In case he comes back?"

"He has only been gone two days, so I'm just not sure you should tear through his stuff."

"I thought you were so sure he was gone for good," Ada said.

Denise nodded halfheartedly. "Okay."

"What, honestly, would he want?"

"It's fine, film there. Just be careful with his things." Ada nodded, and she sat next to her mother on the couch. "What?"

"I need something more," Ada said.

"Yeah?"

"I need to film more of you. Maybe you can go through the archives with me. Maybe—"

"Not right now. No, I don't think I want to do that."

"But Mom, you are all that is left." Denise smiled at Ada. "Think about it."

"I will think about it, honey, but you must give me a little time. And absolutely no filming at the police station. That's too much for me."

"Okay, okay." Ada poured some wine for her mother and then held out her glass. "To Nik, wherever he is."

"To Nik, that selfish prick," Denise said, and started laughing. She took a long sip. She put a hand in Ada's hair and pushed it back from her face. Ada lifted the same section of her hair and tucked it behind her ear. "Do you have any of your film with you? Do you have the Nik interview you did?"

"Oh yeah. Of course. I mean, I have it all with me all the time. I have DVDs in my purse, in my car, everywhere. I can show you the Nik interview if you want to see it."

"I think I would like that."

"Are you sure?"

Ada's camera follows Nik as he walks through his studio and his apartment. There are books to the rafters, shelves everywhere, a drum kit, guitars, recording equipment. Any wall space is covered with notes, photos, charts, drawings. There are no empty spaces, but it looks highly organized. It has the look of systems and purpose. Nik has an unlit cigarette dangling out of his mouth. The camera follows him as he goes outside, walks around the yard, and then they go through the outside entrance to his garage studio.

NIK

That's it, where I have worked the past twenty-four years. Western Lights, the headquarters of Playpen Studios.

ADA *(offscreen)*:

And Pause Collective, and Medium Effort . . .

NIK

Yes, the headquarters of so many record companies. It all happens here, kids.

Nik sits down on a stool and pulls his well-worn Gibson dreadnought guitar onto his lap as he ducks under the strap. We can see rows of the thick black binders of the Chronicles behind him with different years on the spines. Some years get multiple binders.

ADA

You have lived here for how long?

NIK

I moved here in 1981, so close to twenty-four years.

ADA

Do you own it?

He laughs and smiles down at his guitar as he strums a little.

NIK

No, I don't own it. I'm not like your mom and everyone else in this country. I have no desire to take part in the great ownership society.

ADA

Do you consider yourself a political person?

NIK

Not really, I just don't pay attention. I'm too much of a narcissist. I mean, I'll vote against the president this year. I hate the president. But how much do you have to pay attention to realize George Bush is a thug?

ADA

The Chronicles are not just a casual hobby, are they? They are extremely elaborate, the work of a lifetime of effort. They appear to be considered down to the tiniest detail.

NIK

You want to know how detailed? Let's put it this way. If the Chronicles are dug up two hundred years from now, the readers would find them entirely plausible. It would be hard to believe they are conjured from nothing. Particularly when I have all the music. I kept close track. I kept the internal logic and continuity. I have the accompanying scholarship. Verifications could be made.

Nik looks at the volumes lining the shelves. He laughs.

NIK

It isn't just these binders. And the various iterations of recordings. There are movies and videos. There are separate books by some of the characters, there are items of merchandise, there are tie-in promotional products, there are court documents, spin-off projects. I have the collected writings of some of my "reviewers" and so on. Have you ever seen these?

He pulls out a deck of playing cards. Each one has a painting and then writing inked over the painting, sometimes wrapping around to the other side. He shuffles through them.

You remember those *Rock Dreams* books from the seventies? You wouldn't, would you? They were these very popular books. They had dreamy psychedelic paintings of rock stars. Some of the images seemed like lyric illustrations. Others had little stories or poems about the rock star. There were a couple volumes of these books—you were supposed to stare at the paintings while you were listening to the music, I think. They were rock-and-roll-fantasy paintings. Anyway, I thought they were kind of corny, but I also really liked these handmade playing cards I saw, I think maybe at this gallery, ages ago. They were made by Wallace Berman or someone like Wallace Berman. And each card had a poem with a painting or collage on the back. So I stole that idea and combined it with *Rock Dreams.* And I thought the Demonics would release them for their fans as listening decks. Anyway, I made decks for all six of the Demonics records. They are all painted and drawn by hand, no repros. And one edition. I don't know if your mom has even seen these. I think I am the only one who has looked at them, but I have to admit, they are pretty cool. Ha. I am my own biggest fan.

Nik laughs and puts down the cards, then he pulls his guitar in close again.

ADA

But the question is why. Why did you go to such lengths? Can you tell me about why you started keeping the Chronicles?

Nik doesn't say anything, seems to be tuning his guitar. He strums a little.

NIK

It was kind of fun, far away from everyone.

ADA

Is that a lyric from one of your songs? Could you play it?

He sings the song:

NIK

I'm riding static, I hope you hear me
hiding in attics, among old Christmas trees
these widow's flowers, drier than dust
they haven't crumbled, seems that they must

I'm working again, I'm going to break it
I'm playing again, if playing you call it
It happens again, every day
It was kind of fun, so far away . . .
. . . from everyone

I'm riding static, I hope you hear me
hiding in attics, among old Christmas trees
Can't you hear me yet?
Can't you hear me yet?

He has a coughing fit, stops playing, takes a drink of beer.

I know this will be hard to believe, but I just wrote that. (*Laughs.*) It is called "On the Occasion of Being Interviewed for My Niece's Documentary." It is what you call an occasional song.

ADA

Who are you addressing in the song? The world? Yourself? Your sister?

NIK

I'm just making stuff rhyme, and I haven't a clue what it actually means. Interesting, of course, to hear what other people think. I mean, I guess.

ADA

Who is your audience?

NIK

Myself. Other than that, I don't have one, I suppose. Some family and friends.

ADA

My mother.

NIK

For instance.

Nik laughs a big long laugh. Then in a mock theatrical voice:

But sisters don't count. Sorry, Dee Dee. Sisters and mothers don't count, you see. I have no audience.

He strums some more.

Don't mistake me, I don't mean Denise doesn't count in any big sense. My sister doesn't count as my audience because she feels like an extension of me. She's, well, an alternative version of me.

He pauses, reaches offscreen. He takes a drag on his cigarette and exhales. He shrugs.

What were the Chronicles? Accumulations, like memory but better. A thing to look forward to every day.

ADA

But why make a fake life? Why not do it with real life and get a real audience for all your work?

NIK

It wasn't fake, it was real. And I grew to like not having an audience. Imagine being freed from sense and only having to pursue pure sound. Imagine letting go of explanations, of misinterpretations, of commerce and receptions. Imagine doing whatever you want with everything that went before you. Imagine never having to give up Artaud or Chuck Berry or Alistair Crowley or the Beats or the *I Ching* or Lewis Carroll? Imagine total freedom.

ADA

But in your Chronicles you are accused of all of those things. You have your critics call you derivative, immature, and cliché.

NIK

Well, I wanted it to be realistic.

Ada laughs.

You see, *you see*?

He laughs.

> You come at me with your camera and your need for explanations and your wanting me to be consistent.

The film ends. "That's all there is," Ada said. Denise nodded.

Over the next few weeks Denise helped Ada dig through the Chronicles. Denise decided to cooperate fully with the filmmaker. She paid June's rent, and then July's, then August's. She went back to the routine of her life, but many times, instead of going home after work, she would go to Nik's place. She would listen to music or read the Chronicles. Sometimes she thought about her own stack of writing, but mostly she just sat there.

There was no sign of Nik.

After the filming was finished and Ada had returned to New York, Denise didn't come by as often, but she left his apartment and the Chronicles as they were. She liked that there was a space away from her house and her life; she liked being in someone else's world. His apartment felt quiet, disconnected, peaceful.

She visited her mother, who didn't ask about Nik. She saw Jay. They watched movies, they had dinner. Her life felt different, but there were days when it felt exactly the same. The commute. She even went back to watching the news during her dinner.

No one talked about Abu Ghraib or Iraq anymore. All they talked about was Vietnam. They kept showing commercials about how John Kerry was a coward for going to Vietnam, and then they discussed the commercials. The whole election would be decided by Florida, Pennsylvania, and Ohio. The battleground states. Only people in Florida, Pennsylvania, and Ohio would decide if Bush should still be president. Everyone else would just watch. *Not only was I a lurker online, but I lived in a lurker state, California.*

One night in early September, Denise turned on the TV to discover a breaking news story in progress. The words under the image said *school hostage,* and then the words *deadly standoff* zoomed up from the bottom of thc screen. Denise could see the video feed was not an American one. It had that instant rough-grade foreign feel. A reporter spoke, and it was simultaneously translated by a British woman in voice-over. Behind the reporter a large cinder-block building was visible. Then the shot cut to scenes of the building while the American anchor spoke over the images. Denise heard "hundreds of people, reportedly, most of them children." Men with guns were rushing back and forth across the screen. Men in orange jumpsuits carried stretchers into white trucks. People, including children, wandered around unclothed, dazed, damaged. Then the entire screen filled with a map of the former Soviet Union: Russia and all the countries it contained, or used to contain. They cut to a hostage expert sitting on a chair, talking to two reporters sitting next to him. Then a Chechnya expert, then a separatist rebels expert.

The usual news crawl seemed to be suspended; they instead flashed detached facts about Chechnya and Beslan, but it still had the discomforting and discordant effect of too much.

The hostage expert was still speaking. Denise could feel the growing excitement. Something terrible was going to happen. Guaranteed. Glimpses of child hostages next to armed men in balaclavas. They also showed the hard-line, reportedly corrupt Russian police who wouldn't negotiate with a Chechnyan, ever. Villagers, parents, and random passersby—some holding military-grade rifles—also surrounded the building. It was a pending bloodbath, even Denise could see that. And the cable newspeople were besides themselves with how genuinely breaking the news really was. This was one of those rare events that would unfold, dramatically, in real time, right on camera. Denise didn't want to watch it. She didn't even use the remote: she walked up to the TV and pressed its off button. *I won't watch the same things over and over, I won't wait for, hope for, something to happen. I won't.*

But even after the TV turned off, she thought about it. She tried, she really did, to resist her out-of-proportion involvement. She decided she must organize her garage. She went out and pulled all the boxes off the shelves. She made room for new things. She piled all of Jay's gifts into a discreet corner. But something bothered her. It wasn't just the newspeople waiting for the Russian police to storm the school. It wasn't just the serious tone of voice that barely contained a kind of breathless thrill as it said "reportedly wearing suicide bomb belts" and "according to our sources, the rebels say they will kill fifty children for every rebel soldier killed" and "Errol, is it true they are using children as *human shields*?" It wasn't just that concealed giddiness she detected in them, but something else, something in her.

She had an oddly blank feeling—she had a theoretical caring gap. She should be horrified, but she really wasn't. She didn't feel the story seeping into her. Why? Was it because she couldn't see most of the children? That there weren't innocent school photos of them from an earlier time, individual narratives of specific lives told in English with pictures from soccer games? Was it because the school itself looked more like a factory or prison than any school she had ever seen? Or that all of it, the whole thing, felt so deeply foreign? She was afraid that was it, that was what kept her at a remove. There was this secret, shameful feeling that it wasn't quite as bad because it was so foreign. It wasn't as horrifying.

She pushed all the boxes back on the shelves in a neat row and then began to wipe the dust from the empty shelves underneath.

Because, perhaps, they were used to it, in these chaotic foreign countries. They were used to violence and terror and collateral death. Child death. That wasn't true, but it felt true, maybe, how when Americans watched foreign disasters it felt different than watching a school in Colorado, somehow. It was in their clothes, their head scarves, their voices, their full-stop *y*s and *k*s. Even their eyes looked foreign. It felt more like spectacle than she cared to admit.

She had seen the faces of the parents waiting outside. It wasn't them, was it? The war-torn, world-outside-the-USA people weren't inured to bloody children. It was her, watching at home.

When Denise was done, she went into the house. She made dinner. She took a bath and went to bed. She felt tired and quickly fell into a sleep.

When she woke at three a.m., she lay there but knew she wouldn't be able to fall back. She was awake, dreadfully and fully awake. Awful to be awake and alone at this time. The only things were the computer or the TV. She sat up in bed and switched on the cable.

It had happened, the thing they were waiting for, and it was all over the news. *Breaking News* flashed and reflashed across the bottom, but Denise could not take her eyes from the images above it. The school was on fire. She could hear the quick, successive cracks of gunshots. There was a lot of smoke, but she could see people running in all directions. Children were climbing out of windows or being pulled out. Some were bloody, all were naked or nearly naked. Something exploded, and then there were sirens and the men were dumping kids on the grass and going back for more. She could hear crying and yelling. The shot cut to stretchers with small bodies covered completely by white sheets. The newspeople explained the images, but they needed no explanation. The parents were on camera, women with scarves tied on their heads, shrieking in Russian and sobbing. An older woman with a photo of her daughter talked into the camera. The reporter's voice said, "This woman just learned of her daughter's death." Tears streamed down her face, and she held up the picture of her daughter as she bellowed words at the camera. Denise felt her chest catch, and the horror of the thing cascaded all over her. Finally it wasn't, didn't feel, at a distance from her. They were suffering, and the constant presence of suffering made it worse, not easier, didn't it? It was a life that wore on you and weighed on you, and then it kept getting worse. She saw, in the weary, sobbing women, what she recognized as despair. The pain just gets worse.

The Beslan school broke her open, but what purpose did it serve? What was a person supposed to do with all of this feeling? Feeling nothing was subhuman, but feeling everything, like this, in a dark room in the middle of the night, by yourself, did no one any good. Certainly not Denise, who held her head and wept and watched two hours of breaking, beating news coverage. Of children and blood and chaos. Each possibility, *not feeling* or *feeling*, each response was inadequate. Everything was inadequate.

The worst part would come tomorrow, when they repeated these images over and over; or the day after, when the world out there would move to the next thing, the next terrifying and electrifying and stupefying thing. Are we supposed to forget? If not forget, then what?

She couldn't do this anymore. It cost her too much.

A week later, Denise came home from work. She fell asleep easily but woke up well before dawn. She went online and booked a plane ticket to New York. She knew why she did this, and she knew it didn't make sense. She packed a bag and drove herself to the airport in the early-morning dark. She would also visit her daughter. She boarded the plane and sat by the window. She put the tiny paper-covered pillow on the hard plastic between the window hole and the seat. She leaned in to the little scratchy rectangle, closed the window shade, and slept until she arrived in New York.

She didn't have it entirely planned out. When the plane landed, she didn't call Ada. She went to one of the rental car desks. She handed over a credit card. She headed out into the afternoon traffic and made her way to I-87 and drove north.

Denise didn't listen to the radio. She put the last *Ontology* disc in the player, the one he gave her on his birthday. It consisted, as she now knew, not of the antimelodic sound experiments she'd expected. It had nine songs—actual songs—of sad, mostly acoustic music with low, searing vocals. It was, simply, beautiful. It was not dirgy or depressing; it was enigmatic and darkly funny. It was undeniably an end, but an interesting, fecund end that could have been explored for years. Or not.

Denise made it to Albany and stopped to get a sandwich. She drove west on I-90. She followed her map and got off in Canajoharie, a small Mohawk River town with an almost pastoral old-fashioned industrial decay: faded painted signs on brick walls, still-intact stone edifices next to boarded-up windows, and peeling, faintly elegant multipaned storefronts and warehouses. Denise drove slowly through the town, stopped at a gas station for directions, and then headed over a stone bridge past the half-abandoned Beech-Nut factory and into a smaller town, Palatine Bridge. She drove to the Palatine Motel on Route 5 and checked in. It was past eight, and the diner across the road was closed. Denise ate a candy bar and drank some milk. She looked at her map, and then she went to bed. As soon as she turned off the bedside lamp, she fell asleep.

She ate breakfast at the little diner and asked for directions. She drove her rental car up a county road that rose above the river town into the farm hills and woods north of it. The land around her grew empty of homes and businesses. There were high cornfields on either side of the road, but she could still see the hills rising up in the distance. She passed a farmhouse, and then she drove over the crest of a hill. Dead ahead of her she saw a stone church with a tall green wooden steeple. A tiny village was bracketed between the stone church and another church, a plain white clapboard building at the other end of the road. As she drove higher, the hills seemed to fall away from this little road; she could see the foothills of the Adirondacks and the Catskills, and as the sun rose higher in the sky, the whole place seemed to glow—an unusual, quiet, rough-stone glow, but a glow nonetheless. She turned onto the street, and there by the road was a village marker, STONE ARABIA.

Just past the village, she saw a hand-drawn sign that said QUILTS FOR SALE and HONEY FOR SALE. She turned down the long dirt driveway. Denise had asked at the diner about how to find Stone Arabia and the woman and her farm. She said she was looking for a babysitter. Some of the women worked as babysitters for the English. You just had to give them rides.

Denise recognized the house from the images on TV. It was a large white wood farmhouse, with two much larger barns adjacent to it. A man watched her get out of the car. She waved at him. He waved back but didn't smile. She walked over to him, feeling decadent from the smell of exhaust and the weight of her expensive sunglasses. She took off the glasses. He was repairing a piece of farm equipment. He was sweating in black pants, white shirt, and suspenders. He took off his wide-brimmed hat and wiped his head, then put the hat back on. He had a beard and no mustache, as was their custom. Denise had read about all the Old Order rules as she ate breakfast that morning. She had printed a stack of pages from her computer. They believed a mustache was decorative and another opportunity for distracting vanity.

"Good morning," she said.

He nodded. "What can I do for you?"

"I'm looking for a woman. A babysitter."

"Yes."

"Alice Blake." The man nodded. He walked back to the farmhouse and stepped inside. In a few moments, he walked back to her. He pointed over to the house.

"Go to the door that says 'honey for sale.' There, at the back."

"Great, thank you." Denise walked the path to the white farmhouse. The door he pointed to was on a recently built extension. One side had Tyvek insulation sheets nailed to it. Are they allowed to use Dupont-produced Tyvek? But they weren't random Luddites. They just wouldn't use anything that would distract them from their worship of God. Keeping your house warm, up here, was not a luxury. It was a practicality. Denise enjoyed reading about them. They weren't trying to live in the nineteenth century, the way people always think. They were just very cautious and deliberate about technological "innovation." They protect their undistracted life. They are suspicious of progress, improvement, new things. They don't blindly grab at whatever is new. They consider such things with deep skepticism. It wasn't hard to see how much better that might work for someone.

Denise knocked softly on the door, which was unlocked and slightly ajar. She heard someone coming downstairs, and then the door opened and the woman Alice Blake stood before her. She looked like the woman Denise remembered from television, but older. Denise looked into her face—it definitely was the same woman.

"I'm Denise Kranis," she said. "Are you Alice?"

She nodded. "Yes, good to meet you." She gestured for Denise to step into the entryway. It felt very dark after the sunlit yard.

"You are looking for a sitter?" she said.

Denise felt strange and panicked for a moment. She stared at Alice. She shook her head.

"No, not really. That's not true, I'm sorry. I'm very sorry."

Alice's brow twitched and she frowned. She pulled back ever so slightly. She knew why Denise was there. Denise felt her mouth go dry; she hadn't really thought things through.

"What I want to say, what I want to tell you, is I'm so sorry for your loss." Denise could feel her throat constricting as she spoke. "I want to tell you, I want to help you. Find your daughter, I mean. I know they still haven't found anything. If I can help you." Denise felt tears clouding her eyes, and she wiped them. The woman stood there, not moving. There she was, a stranger, so strange, really. *I just wanted to help you. Because, because. How could she know I meant well? Does she think I'm something terrible, a pain tourist?*

The woman could have told her to mind her own business. She could have become angry and told her to leave. But she didn't. She also didn't take Denise's hands and hold them as she uttered a prayer in German. She didn't do that. She didn't start to cry, she didn't say, "Thank you, sister." She didn't do any of those things.

She looked at Denise. Her eyes were very light blue and rimmed in red. Her skin was pale, and Denise could see she actually wasn't very old at all. They stood there for a moment, silently looking at each other. Finally she spoke.

"It is all right. I already know my child is with the Lord."

There was, of course, nothing to be done. She was right. Denise nodded, but didn't move. Alice held the door open. Denise walked through and then turned back to the woman.

"It will be all right," the woman said.

Denise walked to her car, climbed in, and backed out of the long dirt driveway.

She drove down to the city, to Ada, to all that was left.

2006

Sometimes Denise imagined he was in Mexico, with a young wife to take care of him. Maybe he played guitar on a street corner, but that seemed unlikely. If he sold some of his things or if he secretly had stashed some money. It was possible. The police never found out anything.

Denise looked at the link Ada had sent her. Ada's movie, *Garageland,* was long finished, but she had yet to find a distributor. So she posted the film in ten-minute increments on the new video website YouTube. Miraculously, or maybe not, the clips had quickly acquired thousands of hits.

The clips with old Fakes footage had the most hits. And the most comments. But the link Ada sent was for a clip of Denise. She was filmed going through Nik's things, packing them in boxes.

ADA *(offscreen)*

What are you going to do with all of his stuff?

DENISE

Move it to my garage.

ADA

What do you miss most about not having your brother around?

DENISE

It is just . . . knowing someone your whole life—no first impressions, no seductions, no getting to know each other. It is all *know,* at times too much *know.* It is hard to accept, that knowing between us being gone.

She stretched her arm across a stack of boxes. Three rows of stacked boxes were visible behind her.

The disputes, as you age, over what is the true *know,* checking memories against each other, sometimes sweetly, sometimes for a talk, a sorting out, and other times angrily, because all it takes is a hint, a flash of a gun in a jacket, secret and lethal. It is hard to believe that is really gone. *(She pauses, regards the boxes beneath her arm.)* But there is this.

ADA

What remains.

DENISE

And what I remember, of course.

Five thousand hits and counting. People speculated in the comments over who Nik Worth really was. They had theories.

Denise scoured the comments, looking for a clue of some kind. Maybe he was watching from somewhere, it wasn't impossible. Would he love it, the attention, or be annoyed by the inaccuracies about him?

Denise signed up for a user name (DeniseK385) and posted a comment. She corrected some of the factual errors other posters had made about dates, venue names, and other trivia.

Maybe he was in the Netherlands, or Spain.

Maybe he was still in LA, with a new name and a new life. It was even possible that he would contact her at some point. But there was no point in looking for someone who didn't want to be found. She knew he wouldn't be looking back. He wanted to be rid of all of it. Maybe he wanted the freedom to be whatever he wanted to be now, and that required jettisoning all his past work, all his past. He wanted what it was like when he began, before all of it had piled up into a long life.

One day, without trying, Denise ended up near Vista Del Mar and Casa Real, the house they grew up in. She decided to park the car and walk up the street. It looked much nicer than when they had lived there. Each house had been fixed up and painted. The white plaster mission bungalow they used to rent now had a high hedge all the way around it. Denise decided to knock on the door, the way people sometimes do when they see a house they used to live in. She knew it would be a peculiar experience. Memory-palace stuff. Memory palaces were what mnemonic artists used to remember complicated things. Before photos and movies and tape recorders. They would imagine the layout of a building—a palace—either real or invented, and then place things to remember in each room. Then, as they walked through this imaginary house, they would remember what things or ideas they placed on the table or in the cupboard. The hippocampus organized data by some complicated interaction of ideas and spatial associations. The more familiar the building, the better the method worked.

Denise rang the bell. She told the woman who answered she used to live there—grew up there—and would she be so kind as to let her walk through? The memory-palace trick could work the other way, too. Outside of your mind, in the real world. Walk through the place where you used to live, and the details—the ceiling molding, the light from a window, the feel of floorboards as you moved across the threshold of a room—could make you remember everything you did and said and felt in that place, so many years earlier.

1972

Lisa and I are doing our makeup in front of the full-length mirrors attached to my sliding closet doors. We are listening to T. Rex and dancing a little as we do ourselves up. We are laughing, but we are also sort of bored.

I look up and see that Nik is at the door watching us. He has his new Polaroid SX-70. He takes a picture of us in the mirror. I put a hand on my waist and extend the other arm in an exaggerated wave. I wink. I blow a kiss. Lisa puts her arms around my waist and peeks her head through my arm. He takes more pictures. We hear the click and groan as each picture is taken and expelled, and it makes us feel like superstars. He collects each photo as it comes out of the camera and places it on my bed. Nik stops when the film runs out. He pulls out the spent cartridge and chucks it in the wastebasket. He pulls a new pack out of his pocket and clicks it in. He pulls another flash bar out and snaps it on top. I have no idea where he gets the money for all the film and flash bars he uses. But he must use tons: a wall of his room is covered from ceiling to floor with Polaroids. At least half are self-portraits. By the time he has switched film, the posing moment is over, and instead of taking more, we all hover over the photos on the bed, watching as they develop. Something about the flash and the Polaroid film makes a made-up face work particularly well. We are eyes and lips and blush-edged cheekbones. We hardly have noses. We look gorgeous.

"Your album cover," Nik says, pointing to one extra-posey shot. We don't have a band, but we nod in agreement. *That must be the cover*. Now we would have to start a band.

As we stare at the pictures, Nik picks up my eyeliner pencil and approaches the mirror. He stares into his eyes' reflection and grips the pencil.

"Want me to show you?" I say.

"Yeah, but let me do it," he says. I take the pencil and look into the mirror. He watches as I put a finger to my lower lid and pull down. Then I take the hand holding the pencil and apply the tip to the thin strip of skin between eyeball and lash line. I make a dark, smooth line of color. It isn't smudgy at all. It is one of the few things I have mastered in this world—I have the eyeliner business down flat. Nik watches, and then takes the pencil from me and leans close to the mirror. His wide-set eyes are a soft, clear gray, and they look made for augmentation. He shakily applies the liner on one eye and then the other. He blinks at his image.

"You're a prettier girl than I am," I say, and we all laugh, but it's not really a joke. He is. I don't usually look closely at him, but somehow the eyeliner enables a new appraisal. I also notice Lisa is staring at Nik. He's wearing a T-shirt. He's tall and really skinny. It's a tight T-shirt, baby blue with a scoop neck. I realize it is actually one of my T-shirts, and I wonder when my brother decided he needed to get his girl on. But he isn't gay, he is just super vain, and he is currently staring at himself in the mirror, his arms folded.

"Let me take your picture," I say, as if he would ever not let someone take his picture. I pick up his camera and he turns to face me. He starts an apparently well-rehearsed series of poses. He cocks his head, he juts out his jaw slightly and purses his lips. He yawns and looks theatrically bored. He starts to laugh and looks down, hands in pockets. He looks at the camera again, and I notice there is a tiny edge to his expression, an undertone that suggests he is about to do something, or is suppressing something, only you can't quite read it, it might be a smile or a sneer or he might crack up. And he looks as though he is in on the joke somehow, of the phony poses, of his vanity, of a photograph. I can't quite figure out how this works, but I understand that this is what we mean when we say someone looks cool. My brother looks cool. He is wearing my girly T-shirt and eyeliner, and he totally pulls it off.

He stops abruptly and reaches for his camera.

"I can't take this music," he says, and he leaves the room. Lisa and I examine the photos I just took. They move from gray-brown to big blobs of color and then grow sharper.

"Nik is a fox," Lisa says. I shrug. He is so familiar, so deeply of my family life, that it is nearly impossible for me to believe he is sexually attractive to anyone. I fan out the photos. His looks are an abstract asset to me, something I hope reflects my own attractiveness, which I am also blind to. I hold the little padded border of the photos. He could be in a magazine, sure he could. But so could anyone. Nik and I are both theatrical, we both figured out how far that veneer of theater could take you.

We spent many nights alone as little kids. The lack of supervision meant we would have whole evenings of uninterrupted fantasy. We would pretend we were on a ship lost at sea, or were royalty in exile, living in an abandoned country castle (one of Nik's favorites). We were in a musical, and we would burst into song. We were in a bomb shelter, and the whole world had been obliterated. We would lay down the rules of the premise, and we would do what we had to do, make dinner or do chores or whatever, within these made-up parameters. Mama didn't know any of it; by the time she got home from work, she was just glad we were safe and fed and in bed. As we got older, we retained our love of artifice of any kind. Nik's first stab at a band was called the Make-Believers.

I revel in affectation and teach it to Lisa. Even if I weren't already an expert, it wouldn't take a girl long to figure it out. All you have to do is put on your clothes and makeup and go for a walk on lower Sunset, where all the clubs are, or even just waltz into Hamburger Hamlet: we would get looks, we would get attention. It's fun because we are made up—not just in makeup, but we are made-up, imaginary people. We are liberated because not only do we know we can pull it off (whatever it is) but we know everyone else is a fake, too. Maybe Lisa doesn't yet know this, but I have always known it.

We decide to get Nik to drive us over to Sunset. We live not far away, but we don't want to trudge the back blocks in our high heels. Besides, Nik is a good accessory. He always knows what club has good music and is always being invited to parties. If I look iffy and maybe a bit too young, Nik tips the scales in my favor; he ups the charade considerably. You might ask what the goal of all of this is, but believe me, it is pretty innocent. We don't have sex, not yet, and we rarely drink much or do any drugs (Nik, alas, is a different story). We just want to be out and around the sex and drugs, the hip adults; we want to hear good music, and we want—most of all—to be looked at and desired. We want to feel that desire the way you feel the hot sun burning down on your head. We want it to cover us and make us glow. That is enough for me, anyway.

I pound on his door. Our walls and doors, his and mine, are covered in posters. The door to his room has a huge poster of Lou Reed's new album *Transformer.* Reed has an angular face, prominent ears, and a lot of eye makeup on. He looks like a dainty version of Frankenstein. Now I grasp what Nik is getting at with his ragged drag.

He opens the door. He has augmented my T-shirt with an ancient yellow chiffon scarf. He is smoking a joint. He gives us an exaggerated look of fatigue. Lisa giggles with longing as I propose he take us out. He considers and shrugs.

"I left a note for Ma," I say. That is all we have to do, since she works the night shift. She doesn't usually come back until about three, but we might want to stay out even later, so we leave a note. It sounds remarkably unsupervised, doesn't it? And it is, but it has always been like that. She works at a call center, an answering service. She has for years. Way back, when our father was still around, Nik would go to his house after school, and I would actually go to work with my mother. They let her bring me, and I would sit under her desk most of the time, eat my sandwich, draw or color, and eventually fall asleep in my sleeping bag. I loved it. I remember looking at my mother's soft legs in nude stockings and low-heeled pumps. She always had these chubby legs. She hated them and wore long skirts to hide them, but I loved those legs, loved being near them. She would wake me up at two, then I would sleepwalk to the car. I'd sleep on the ride home. Usually I wouldn't even remember her finally tucking me into bed. I didn't mind it at all—I tried to be as portable as possible. She used to call me her pocket kid. But that didn't last for too long. My father left town again, and Nik and I settled into our routine on our own. In the morning she sleeps while we get ourselves up for school. I make my own breakfast (blueberry Pop-Tart with vanilla frosting). Nik always just has coffee with tons of sugar. We made ourselves into little adults, and we have oh-so-much freedom.

Nik took us out in his purple 1967 Chevy Nova. It was kind of a shit car, but it was a cool shit car. Nick got it cheap, he spent all last summer working as a busboy until he had the money. He quit the job, and now it is a bit of a mystery where he gets his spending money, but I have a few guesses. Like my mom, I pretend not to think about it. We are all really good at pretending we are a normal family, and somehow us pretending all at once is a big part of what makes us feel like a family. It is like a willed self-delusion. Or maybe you can lie to yourself, that's a self-delusion, but if you have a delusion about several people, if you all share in this delusion, that isn't a self-delusion, is it? That is a family.

The car is a necessity. We get in, roll down all the windows, and play the radio loud. We all light cigarettes. We drive around. Nothing is really going on. We are bored. We end up at a stupid party for rich high school kids in Westwood. I see no one I want to talk to and I think it is a horrible scene, but then I notice Nik making out with a little blond girl. She's on his lap, and I can tell by the way they are interlacing their fingers and then staring at them that they have taken acid. I sigh.

"Call your mom to come pick us up," I say to Lisa. She nods. We leave Nik there.

When I open the door, I collapse a little at the thought of the empty house. Without my mother or Nik, I feel more alone than frightened, and I quickly turn on the TV to hear something besides my own breathing. The house is small, low-ceilinged, and contained. I walk through the kitchen to the back door. I walk to the garage, which has become Nik's studio. I use the hidden spare key, open the side door, and snap on the light. Nik has a couch covered by one of our old thick chenille bedspreads. It is the perfect place to sit and listen to music. He has a pretty good stereo and a set of excellent headphones. He has a makeshift coffee table with a board set on top of it. The board is full of ink marks. Nik likes to sit at the table and draw while he listens to the music. His ink drawings cover the ceiling. Most of them are his album covers. He always draws himself the same, as Nik Kat, his alter ego from his zine days, now grown up, a tall skinny man with a cat head. The style is very *Comix,* but old-timey-looking, like WWII propaganda cartoons. Nik Kat's stock pose is bent back from the stomach, as if he has just been punched. His ever-present cigarette is in midair in front of his open mouth. The eyes bug, the hat flies up. I have no idea why Nik depicts himself that way. But Nik Kat is everywhere, even if he is only a little figure in the corner of a larger work. The walls of the garage are lined in carpet pieces to muffle sound. I sit on the couch. It smells of incense and pot and cigarettes. But the place is actually quite orderly and neat. Nik is not a slob. Every surface is covered, but it looks good, it all works and creates a little world. The part of the garage opposite the couch has the band area: guitars, drum kit, keyboard. There is a microphone and some small amplifiers. The ink drawings on the ceiling, the walls with the carpet pieces, the gear—it all looks great somehow. All the layers and odd juxtapositions—it is as if everything in his head splays out onto the walls.

I look for cigarettes in the set of drawers by the couch. He has three copies of a Peter Max poster side by side on the back wall. They are mounted on cardboard and tacked into the carpet. They have lots of pink and blue rainbows and stars, and a huge Pan Am 747 flying away from an earthlike head. If Nik likes something, he can't get enough of it. Sometimes he repeats things exactly, sometimes with a slight variation. I dunno, I think it is like verse-chorus-verse-chorus. Or how you really love a song after you've heard it over and over, how your body feels almost desperate for the next part.

He keeps his records in a row, not in alphabetical order, but in an order based on Nik's very personal and constantly changing categories. He calls his system idiosyncratic. He looked it up in the dictionary, and it comes from the Greek word for *private* and the Greek word for *mixture*. So the categories are Nik's private mix of concerns. Which means not my concern, I guess, or *Go ahead and try to figure it out*. I turn on the stereo, drop the needle on the record by some band I never heard of. I listen to the chiming acoustic guitar, the gentle-boy vocal, the sweet harmonies. The lyrics are childlike and innocent, but there is a little edge of want under it that feels kind of sexy. It is hard not to wish for a boyfriend who would sing like this. The song ends with a sloppy dribble out and then slips right into a hard electric guitar riff. The next song isn't slow or sweet, but the singer likes to slur the words, mangle them until he sounds almost deranged with want. Like he can't quite get it together because he has it so bad for this girl. Then he's back to singing a slow song, and he's hurting, sad, his voice is cracking, and then, yikes, there are even some string instruments, a kind of orchestration. He almost loses me, but just at that moment the harmonies overwhelm the strings and the next tough-sweet guitar riff comes in. I am won—all of it, even the dreaded violins. Now I really feel something: love, sure, need, sure, even hurt, just everything all at once for these guys. I look at the album cover. I lie on the couch. I turn it up. Totally ordinary-looking, but I want one for a boyfriend. Just one word-tripping sloppy boy who I could make stammer and beg. But with harmonies and melody and all those angelic high notes. I start the slow song again. That voice, I can't explain how much it fits with what I am feeling, what I want and need, alone in the garage. I start to sing along and I feel something else: I feel like I am him, this is *my* little edge of want. So I want to be the voice and I want to be the one the voice wants. All of it at once. *I want it so bad.*

AUTHOR'S NOTE

Although this novel is a work of fiction and Nik Worth is a character of my imagination, my inspiration for him is a real-life person, my stepfather, Richard Frasca, a.k.a. Jon Denmar. Richard Frasca is not Nik Worth, but Richard's devotion to his own music and Richard's self-documented chronicle of his life as a secret rock star gave me the idea for Nik. Thank you, Richard, for your generosity. You are a true artist. Viva Village.

ACKNOWLEDGMENTS

I want to thank the John Simon Guggenheim Memorial Foundation for supporting my work. Thank you to the American Academy of Arts and Letters and the American Academy in Rome. Thank you to the New York Foundation for the Arts. This book would not have been possible without the help of these foundations.

Clement Coleman helped me write the lyrics to "On the Occasion of Being Interviewed for My Niece's Documentary." Clem also let me take his titles *Breakfast at Kingdom Come* and *Meet Me at the Movies*. Thank you for constantly inspiring me with your hardworking songwriting ways. I also want to thank Emy and Kathy Frasca. I'm indebted to the many people who helped answer my questions: Marna Nape, Katherine Waterson, David Humphrey, Kurt Rohde, Keeril Makan, Dwynn Golden, Patrick Williams, Shahram Victory, and Martin Brody. Thank you to George Andreou, Rick Moody, and André Bernard. Thank you to everyone at the Syracuse University Creative Writing Program.

As always, I am deeply grateful for the generous support of Nan Graham, Melanie Jackson, and Don DeLillo.